THE THIRD MAN

LOSER TAKES ALL

ALSO BY
GRAHAM GREENE

NOVELS

The Man Within · Orient Express (Stamboul Train)
It's a Battlefield · The Shipwrecked (England Made Me)
Brighton Rock · The Power and the Glory
The Heart of the Matter
The End of the Affair · This Gun for Hire (A Gun for Sale)
The Confidential Agent · The Ministry of Fear
The Quiet American
Our Man in Havana · A Burnt-Out Case · The Comedians
Travels with my Aunt · The Honorary Consul
The Human Factor · Doctor Fischer of Geneva or The Bomb Party

SHORT STORIES

Collected Stories
(including *Twenty-one Stories, A Sense of Reality,*
and *May We Borrow Your Husband?*)

TRAVEL

Journey Without Maps
Another Mexico (The Lawless Roads)
In Search of a Character

ESSAYS

Collected Essays
The Pleasure Dome
British Dramatists

PLAYS

The Living Room
The Potting Shed
The Complaisant Lover
Carving a Statue
The Return of A. J. Raffles

AUTOBIOGRAPHY

A Sort of Life
Ways of Escape

BIOGRAPHY

Lord Rochester's Monkey

Graham Greene

THE THIRD MAN

LOSER TAKES ALL

THE VIKING PRESS
NEW YORK

The Third Man

Copyright © 1949 by Graham Greene
Copyright renewed © 1976 by Graham Greene
First published in 1950 by The Viking Press

Loser Takes All

Copyright © 1954 by Graham Greene
Copyright renewed © 1982 by Graham Greene
First published in 1957 by The Viking Press

Both titles reissued in 1983 by The Viking Press
40 West 23rd Street, New York, N.Y. 10010

ISBN 0-670-70084-3

Printed in the United States of America
Set in Monotype Plantin Light

THE THIRD MAN

[1]

One never knows when the blow may fall. When I saw Rollo Martins first I made this note on him for my security police files: 'In normal circumstances a cheerful fool. Drinks too much and may cause a little trouble. Whenever a woman passes raises his eyes and makes some comment, but I get the impression that really he'd rather not be bothered. Has never really grown up and perhaps that accounts for the way he worshipped Lime.' I wrote there that phrase 'in normal circumstances' because I met him first at Harry Lime's funeral. It was February, and the gravediggers had been forced to use electric drills to open the frozen ground in Vienna's Central Cemetery. It was as if even nature were doing its best to reject Lime, but we got him in at last and laid the earth back on him like bricks. He was vaulted in, and Rollo Martins walked quickly away as though his long gangly legs wanted to break into a run, and the tears of a boy ran down his thirty-five-year-old face. Rollo Martins believed in friendship, and that was why what happened later was a worse shock to him than it would have been to you or me (you because you would have put it down to an illusion and me because at once a rational explanation – however wrongly – would have come to my mind). If only he had come to tell me then, what a lot of trouble would have been saved.

If you are to understand this strange, rather sad story you must have an impression at least of the background – the smashed dreary city of Vienna divided up in zones among the Four Powers – the Russian, the British, the American, the French zones, regions marked only by notice boards, and in the centre of the city, surrounded by the Ring with its heavy public buildings and its prancing statuary, the Innere Stadt under the control of all Four Powers. In this once fashionable Inner City each power in turn, for a month at a time, takes, as we call it, 'the chair', and becomes responsible for security; at night, if you were fool enough to waste your Austrian schillings on a night club, you would be fairly certain to see the International Power at work – four military police, one from each power, communicating with each other, if they communicated at all, in the common language of their enemy. I never knew Vienna between the wars, and I am too young to remember the old Vienna with its Strauss music and its bogus easy charm; to me it is simply a city of undignified ruins which turned that February into great glaciers of snow and ice. The Danube was a grey flat muddy river a long way off across the Second Bezirk, the Russian zone where the Prater lay smashed and desolate and full of weeds, only the Great Wheel revolving slowly over the foundations of merry-go-rounds like abandoned millstones, the rusting iron of smashed tanks which nobody had cleared away, the frost-nipped weeds where the snow was thin. I haven't enough imagination to picture it as it had once been, any more than I can picture Sacher's Hotel as other than a transit hotel for English officers or see the Kärntnerstrasse as a fashionable shopping street instead of a street which exists, most of it, only at eye level, repaired up to the first storey. A Russian soldier in a fur cap goes by with a rifle over his shoulder, a few tarts cluster round the American Information Office, and men in overcoats sip ersatz coffee in the windows of the Old Vienna. At night it is just as well to stick to the Inner City or the zones of three of the Powers, though even there the kidnappings occur – such senseless kidnappings they sometimes seemed to us – a Ukrainian girl without a passport, an old man beyond the age of usefulness, sometimes, of course, the technician or the traitor. This was roughly the Vienna to which Rollo Martins came on February seventh last year. I have reconstructed the affair as best I can from my own files and from what Martins told me. It is as accurate as I can make it – I have tried not to invent a line of dialogue, though I can't vouch for Martins' memory; an ugly story if you leave out the girl: grim and sad and un-relieved, if it were not for that absurd episode of the British Council lecturer.

[2]

A British subject can still travel if he is content to take with him only five English pounds which he is forbidden to spend abroad, but if Rollo Martins had not received an invitation from Lime of the International Refugee Office he would not have been allowed to enter Austria, which counts still as occupied territory. Lime had suggested that Martins might write up the business of looking after the international refugees, and although it wasn't Martins' usual line, he had consented. It would give him a holiday, and he badly needed a holiday after the inci-dent in Dublin and the other incident in Amsterdam; he always tried to dismiss women as 'incidents', things that simply happened to him without any will of his own, acts of God in the eyes of insurance agents. He had a haggard look when he arrived in Vienna and a habit of looking over his shoulder that for a time made me suspicious of him until I realized that he went in fear that one of, say, six people might turn up unexpectedly. He told me vaguely that he had been mixing his drinks – that was another way of putting it.

Rollo Martins' usual line was the writing of cheap paper-covered Westerns under the name of Buck Dexter. His public was large but unremunerative. He couldn't have afforded Vienna if Lime had not offered to pay his expenses when he got there out of some vaguely described propaganda fund. Lime could also, he said, keep him supplied with paper bafs – the only currency in use from a penny upwards in British hotels and clubs. So it was with exactly five unusable pound notes that Martins arrived in Vienna.

An odd incident had occurred at Frankfurt, where the plane from London grounded for an hour. Martins was eating a hamburger in the American canteen (a kindly airline supplied the passengers with a voucher for sixty-five cents' worth of food) when a man he could recognize from twenty feet away as a journalist approached his table.

'You Mr Dexter?' he asked.

'Yes,' Martins said, taken off his guard.

'You look younger than your photographs,' the man said. 'Like to make a statement? I represent the local forces paper here. We'd like to know what you think of Frankfurt.'

'I only touched down ten minutes ago.'

'Fair enough,' the man said. 'What about views on the American novel?'

'I don't read them,' Martins said.

'The well-known acid humour,' the journalist said.

14

He pointed at a small grey-haired man with protruding teeth, nibbling a bit of bread. 'Happen to know if that's Carey?'

'No. What Carey?'

'J. G. Carey of course.'

'I've never heard of him.'

'You novelists live out of the world. He's my real assignment,' and Martins watched him make across the room for the great Carey, who greeted him with a false headline smile, laying down his crust. Dexter wasn't the man's assignment, but Martins couldn't help feeling a certain pride – nobody had ever before referred to him as a novelist; and that sense of pride and importance carried him over the disappointment when Lime was not there to meet him at the airport. We never get accustomed to being less important to other people than they are to us – Martins felt the little jab of dispensability, standing by the bus door, watching the snow come sifting down, so thinly and softly that the great drifts among the ruined buildings had an air of permanence, as though they were not the result of this meagre fall, but lay, for ever, above the line of perpetual snow.

There was no Lime to meet him at the Hotel Astoria, the terminus where the bus landed him, and no message – only a cryptic one for Mr Dexter from someone he had never heard of called Crabbin. 'We expected you on to-morrow's plane. Please stay where you are. On the way round. Hotel room booked.' But Rollo Martins wasn't the kind of man who stayed around. If you stayed around in a hotel lounge, sooner or later incidents occurred; one mixed one's drinks. I can hear Rollo Martins saying to me, 'I've done with incidents. No more incidents,' before he plunged head first into the most serious incident of all. There was always a conflict in Rollo Martins – between the absurd Christian name and the sturdy Dutch (four generations back) surname. Rollo looked at every woman that passed, and Martins renounced them for ever. I don't know which one of them wrote the Westerns.

Martins had been given Lime's address and he felt no curiosity about the man called Crabbin; it was too obvious that a mistake had been made, though he didn't yet connect it with the conversation at Frankfurt. Lime had written that he could put Martins up in his own flat, a large apartment on the edge of Vienna that had been requisitioned from a Nazi owner. Lime could pay for the taxi when he arrived, so Martins drove straight away to the building lying in the third (British) zone. He kept the taxi waiting while he mounted to the third floor.

How quickly one becomes aware of silence even in so silent a city as Vienna with the snow steadily settling. Martins hadn't reached the second floor before he was convinced that he would not find Lime there, but the silence was deeper than just absence – it was as if he would not find Lime anywhere in Vienna, and, as he reached the third floor and saw the big black bow over the door handle, anywhere in the world at all. Of course it might have been a cook who had died, a housekeeper, anybody but Harry Lime, but he knew – he felt he had known twenty stairs down – that Lime, the Lime he had hero-worshipped now for twenty years, since the first meeting in a grim school corridor with a cracked bell ringing for prayers, was gone. Martins wasn't wrong, not entirely wrong. After he had rung the bell half a dozen times a small man with a sullen expression put his head out from another flat and told him in a tone of vexation, 'It's no use. There's nobody there. He's dead.'

'Herr Lime ?'

'Herr Lime, of course.'

Martins said to me later, 'At first it didn't mean a thing. It was just a bit of information, like those paragraphs in *The Times* they call "News in Brief". I said to him, "When did it happen ? How ?"'

'He was run over by a car,' the man said. 'Last Thursday.' He added sullenly, as if really this were none of his business, 'They're burying him this afternoon. You've only just missed them.'

'Them ?'

'Oh, a couple of friends and the coffin.'

'Wasn't he in hospital ?'

'There was no sense in taking him to hospital. He was killed here on his own doorstep – instantaneously. The right-hand mudguard struck him on his shoulder and bowled him over like a rabbit.'

It was only then, Martins told me, when the man used the word 'rabbit', that the dead Harry Lime came alive, became the boy with a gun which he had shown Martins the means of 'borrowing'; a boy starting up among the long sandy burrows of Brickworth Common saying, 'Shoot, you fool, shoot! There,' and the rabbit limped to cover, wounded by Martins' shot.

'Where are they burying him ?' he asked the stranger on the landing.

'In the Central Cemetery. They'll have a hard time of it in this frost.'

He had no idea how to pay for his taxi, or indeed where in Vienna he could find a room in which he could live for five English pounds, but that problem had to be postponed until he had seen the last of Harry Lime. He drove straight out of town into the suburb (British zone) where the Central Cemetery lay. One passed through the Russian zone to reach it, and took a short cut through the American zone, which you couldn't mistake because of the ice-cream parlours in every street. The trams ran along the high wall of the Central Cemetery, and for a mile on the other side of the rails stretched the monumental masons and the market gardeners – an apparently endless chain of gravestones waiting for owners and wreaths waiting for mourners.

Martins had not realized the size of this huge snowbound park where he was making his last rendezvous with Lime. It was as if Harry had left a message for him, 'Meet me in Hyde Park', without specifying a spot between the Achilles statue and Lancaster Gate; the avenues of graves, each avenue numbered and lettered, stretched out like the spokes of an enormous wheel; they drove for a half-mile towards the west, and then turned and drove a half-mile north, turned south. . . . The snow gave the great pompous family headstones an air of grotesque comedy; a toupée of snow slipped sideways over an angelic face, a saint wore a heavy white moustache, and a shako of snow tipped at a drunken angle over the bust of a superior civil servant called Wolfgang Gottmann. Even this cemetery was zoned between the Powers: the Russian zone was marked by huge tasteless statues of armed men, the French by rows of anonymous wooden crosses and a torn tired tricolour flag. Then Martins remembered that Lime was a Catholic and was unlikely to be buried in the British zone for which they had been vainly searching. So back they drove through the heart of a forest where the graves

18

lay like wolves under the trees, winking white eyes under the gloom of the evergreens. Once from under the trees emerged a group of three men in strange eighteenth-century black and silver uniforms with three-cornered hats pushing a kind of barrow: they crossed a ride in the forest of graves and disappeared again.

It was just chance that they found the funeral in time – one patch in the enormous park where the snow had been shovelled aside and a tiny group was gathered, apparently bent on some very private business. A priest had finished speaking, his words coming secretively through the thin patient snow, and a coffin was on the point of being lowered into the ground. Two men in lounge suits stood at the graveside; one carried a wreath that he obviously had forgotten to drop on to the coffin, for his companion nudged his elbow so that he came to with a start and dropped the flowers. A girl stood a little way away with her hands over her face, and I stood twenty yards away by another grave, watching with relief the last of Lime and noticing carefully who was there – just a man in a mackintosh I was to Martins. He came up to me and said, 'Could you tell me who they are burying?'

'A fellow called Lime,' I said, and was astonished to see the tears start to this stranger's eyes: he didn't look like a man who wept, nor was Lime the kind of man whom I thought likely to have mourners – genuine mourners with genuine tears. There was the girl of course, but one excepts women from all such generalizations.

Martins stood there, till the end, close beside me. He said to me later that as an old friend he didn't want to intrude on these newer ones – Lime's death belonged to them, let them have it. He was under the sentimental illusion that Lime's life – twenty years of it anyway – belonged to him. As soon as the affair was over – I am not a religious man and always feel a little impatient with the fuss that surrounds death – Martins strode away on his long legs, which always seemed likely to get entangled together, back to his taxi. He made no attempt to speak to anyone, and the tears now were really running, at any rate the few meagre drops that any of us can squeeze out at our age.

One's file, you know, is never quite complete; a case is never really closed, even after a century, when all the participants are dead. So I followed Martins: I knew the other three: I wanted to know the stranger. I caught him up by his taxi and said, 'I haven't any transport. Would you give me a lift into town?'

'Of course,' he said. I knew the driver of my jeep would spot me as we came out and follow us unobtrusively. As we drove away I noticed Martins never looked behind – it's nearly always the fake mourners and the fake lovers who take that last look, who wait waving on platforms, instead of clearing quickly out, not looking back. Is it perhaps that they love themselves so much and want to keep themselves in the sight of others, even of the dead?

I said, 'My name's Calloway.'

'Martins,' he said.

'You were a friend of Lime?'

'Yes.' Most people in the last week would have hesitated before they admitted quite so much.

'Been here long?'

'I only came this afternoon from England. Harry had asked me to stay with him. I hadn't heard.'

'Bit of a shock?'

'Look here,' he said. 'I badly want a drink, but I haven't any cash – except five pounds sterling. I'd be awfully grateful if you'd stand me one.'

It was my turn to say 'Of course'. I thought for a moment and told the driver the name of a small bar in the Kärntnerstrasse. I didn't think he'd want to be seen for a while in a busy British bar full of transit officers and their wives. This bar – perhaps because it was exorbitant in its prices – seldom had more than one self-occupied couple in it at a time. The trouble was too that it really only had one drink – a sweet chocolate liqueur that the waiter improved at a price with cognac – but I got the impression that Martins had no objection to any drink so long as it cast a veil over the present and the past. On the door was the usual notice saying the bar opened from six till ten, but one just pushed the door and walked through the front rooms. We had a whole small room to ourselves; the only couple were next door, and the waiter, who knew me, left us alone with some caviare sandwiches. It was lucky that we both knew I had an expense account.

Martins said over his second quick drink, 'I'm sorry, but he was the best friend I ever had.'

I couldn't resist saying, knowing what I knew, and because I was anxious to vex him – one learns a lot that way – 'That sounds like a cheap novelette.'

He said quickly, 'I write cheap novelettes.'

I had learned something anyway. Until he had had a third drink I was under the impression that he wasn't an easy talker, but I felt fairly certain he was one of those who turn unpleasant after their fourth glass.

I said, 'Tell me about yourself – and Lime.'

'Look here,' he said, 'I badly need another drink, but I

can't keep on scrounging on a stranger. Could you change me a pound or two into Austrian money?'

'Don't bother about that,' I said and called the waiter. 'You can treat me when I come to London on leave. You were going to tell me how you met Lime?'

The glass of chocolate liqueur might have been a crystal, the way he looked at it and turned it this way and that. He said, 'It was a long time ago. I don't suppose anyone knows Harry the way I do,' and I thought of the thick file of agents' reports in my office, each claiming the same thing. I believe in my agents; I've sifted them all very thoroughly.

'How long?'

'Twenty years – or a bit more. I met him my first term at school. I can see the place. I can see the notice board and what was on it. I can hear the bell ringing. He was a year older and knew the ropes. He put me wise to a lot of things.' He took a quick dab at his drink and then turned the crystal again as if to see more clearly what there was to see. He said, 'It's funny. I can't remember meeting any woman quite as well.'

'Was he clever at school?'

'Not the way they wanted him to be. But what things he did think up! He was a wonderful planner. I was far better at subjects like History and English than Harry, but I was a hopeless mug when it came to carrying out his plans.' He laughed: he was already beginning, with the help of drink and talk, to throw off the shock of the death. He said, 'I was always the one who got caught.'

'That was convenient for Lime.'

'What the hell do you mean?' he asked. Alcoholic irritation was setting in.

'Well, wasn't it?'

'That was my fault, not his. He could have found someone cleverer if he'd chosen, but he liked me.' Certainly, I thought, the child is father to the man, for I too had found Lime patient.

'When did you see him last?'

'Oh, he was over in London six months ago for a medical congress. You know, he qualified as a doctor, though he never practised. That was typical of Harry. He just wanted to see if he could do a thing and then he lost interest. But he used to say that it often came in handy.' And that too was true. It was odd how like the Lime he knew was to the Lime I knew: it was only that he looked at Lime's image from a different angle or in a different light. He said, 'One of the things I liked about Harry was his humour.' He gave a grin which took five years off his age. 'I'm a buffoon. I like playing the silly fool, but Harry had real wit. You know, he could have been a first-class light composer if he had worked at it.'

He whistled a tune – it was oddly familiar to me. 'I always remember that. I saw Harry write it. Just in a couple of minutes on the back of an envelope. That was what he always whistled when he had something on his mind. It was his signature tune.' He whistled the tune a second time, and I knew then who had written it – of course it wasn't Harry. I nearly told him so, but what was the point? The tune wavered and went out. He stared down into his glass, drained what was left, and said, 'It's a damned shame to think of him dying the way he did.'

'It was the best thing that ever happened to him,' I said.

He didn't take in my meaning at once: he was a little hazy with his drinks. 'The best thing?'

'Yes.'

'You mean there wasn't any pain?'

'He was lucky in that way, too.'

It was my tone of voice and not my words that caught Martins' attention. He asked gently and dangerously – I could see his right hand tighten – 'Are you hinting at something?'

There is no point at all in showing physical courage in all situations: I eased my chair far enough back to be out of reach of his fist. I said, 'I mean that I had his case completed at police headquarters. He would have served a long spell – a very long spell – if it hadn't been for the accident.'

'What for?'

'He was about the worst racketeer who ever made a dirty living in this city.'

I could see him measuring the distance between us and deciding that he couldn't reach me from where he sat. Rollo wanted to hit out, but Martins was steady, careful. Martins, I began to realize, was dangerous. I wondered whether after all I had made a complete mistake: I couldn't see Martins being quite the mug that Rollo had made out. 'You're a policeman?' he asked.

'Yes.'

'I've always hated policemen. They are always either crooked or stupid.'

'Is that the kind of book you write?'

I could see him edging his chair round to block my way out. I caught the waiter's eye and he knew what I meant – there's an advantage in always using the same bar for interviews.

Martins brought out a surface smile and said gently, 'I have to call them sheriffs.'

'Been in America?' It was a silly conversation.

'No. Is this an interrogation?'

'Just interest.'

'Because if Harry was that kind of racketeer, I must be one too. We always worked together.'

'I daresay he meant to cut you in – somewhere in the organization. I wouldn't be surprised if he had meant to give you the baby to hold. That was his method at school – you told me, didn't you? And, you see, the headmaster was getting to know a thing or two.'

'You are running true to form, aren't you? I suppose there was some petty racket going on with petrol and you couldn't pin it on anyone, so you've picked a dead man. That's just like a policeman. You're a real policeman, I suppose?'

'Yes, Scotland Yard, but they've put me into a colonel's uniform when I'm on duty.'

He was between me and the door now. I couldn't get away from the table without coming into range. I'm no fighter, and he had six inches of advantage anyway. I said, 'It wasn't petrol.'

'Tyres, saccharin – why don't you policemen catch a few murderers for a change?'

'Well, you could say that murder was part of his racket.'

He pushed the table over with one hand and made a dive at me with the other; the drink confused his calculations. Before he could try again my driver had his arms round him. I said, 'Don't treat him rough. He's only a writer with too much drink in him.'

'Be quiet, can't you, sir,' my driver said. He had an exaggerated sense of officer-class. He would probably have called Lime 'sir'.

'Listen, Callaghan, or whatever your bloody name is . . .'

'Calloway. I'm English, not Irish.'

'I'm going to make you look the biggest bloody fool in Vienna. There's one dead man you aren't going to pin your unsolved crimes on.'

'I see. You're going to find me the real criminal? It sounds like one of your stories.'

'You can let me go, Callaghan. I'd rather make you look the fool you are than black your bloody eye. You'd only have to go to bed for a few days with a black eye. But when I've finished with you, you'll leave Vienna.'

I took out a couple of pounds' worth of bafs and stuck them in his breast pocket. 'These will see you through tonight,' I said, 'and I'll make sure they keep a seat for you on tomorrow's London plane.'

'You can't turn me out. My papers are in order.'

'Yes, but this is like other cities: you need money here. If you change your sterling on the black market I'll catch up on you inside twenty-four hours. Let him go.'

Rollo Martins dusted himself down. He said, 'Thanks for the drinks.'

'That's all right.'

'I'm glad I don't have to feel grateful. I suppose they were on expenses?'

'Yes.'

'I'll be seeing you again in a week or two when I've got the dope.' I knew he was angry. I didn't believe then that he was serious. I thought he was putting over an act to cheer up his self-esteem.

'I might come and see you off tomorrow.'

'I shouldn't waste your time. I won't be there.'

'Paine here will show you the way to Sacher's. You

can get a bed and dinner there. I'll see to that.'

He stepped to one side as though to make way for the waiter and slashed out at me. I just avoided him, but stumbled against the table. Before he could try again Paine had landed him one on the mouth. He went bang over in the alleyway between the tables and came up bleeding from a cut lip. I said, 'I thought you promised not to fight.'

He wiped some of the blood away with his sleeve and said, 'Oh, no, I said I'd rather make you a bloody fool. I didn't say I wouldn't give you a black eye as well.'

I had had a long day and I was tired of Rollo Martins. I said to Paine, 'See him safely into Sacher's. Don't hit him again if he behaves,' and turning away from both of them towards the inner bar (I deserved one more drink), I heard Paine say respectfully to the man he had just knocked down, 'This way, sir. It's only just around the corner.'

[3]

What happened next I didn't hear from Paine but from Martins a long time afterwards, as I reconstructed the chain of events which did indeed – though not quite in the way he had expected – prove me to be a fool. Paine simply saw him to the head porter's desk and explained there, 'This gentleman came in on the plane from London. Colonel Calloway says he's to have a room.' Having made that clear, he said, 'Good evening, sir,' and left. He was probably a bit embarrassed by Martins' bleeding lip.

'Had you already got a reservation, sir?' the porter asked.

'No. No, I don't think so,' Martins said in a muffled voice, holding his handkerchief to his mouth.

'I thought perhaps you might be Mr Dexter. We had a room reserved for a week for Mr Dexter.'

Martins said, 'Oh, I am Mr Dexter.' He told me later that it occurred to him that Lime might have engaged a room for him in that name because perhaps it was Buck Dexter and not Rollo Martins who was to be used for propaganda purposes. A voice said at his elbow, 'I'm so sorry you were not met at the plane, Mr Dexter. My name's Crabbin.'

The speaker was a stout middle-aged young man with a natural tonsure and one of the thickest pairs of horn-rimmed glasses that Martins had ever seen. He went apologetically on, 'One of our chaps happened to ring up Frankfurt and heard you were on the plane. H.Q. made one of their usual foolish mistakes and wired you were not coming. Something about Sweden, but the cable was badly mutilated. Directly I heard from Frankfurt I tried to meet the plane, but I just missed you. You got my note?'

Martins held his handkerchief to his mouth and said obscurely, 'Yes. Yes?'

'May I say at once, Mr Dexter, how excited I am to meet you?'

'Good of you.'

'Ever since I was a boy, I've thought you the greatest novelist of our century.'

Martins winced. It was painful opening his mouth to protest. He took an angry look instead at Mr Crabbin, but it was impossible to suspect that young man of a practical joke.

'You have a big Austrian public, Mr Dexter, both for

28

your originals and your translations. Especially for *The Curved Prow*, that's my own favourite.'

Martins was thinking hard. 'Did you say – room for a week?'

'Yes.'

'Very kind of you.'

'Mr Schmidt here will give you tickets every day, to cover all meals. But I expect you'll need a little pocket money. We'll fix that. Tomorrow we thought you'd like a quiet day – to look about.'

'Yes.'

'Of course any of us are at your service if you need a guide. Then the day after tomorrow in the evening there's a little quiet discussion at the Institute – on the contemporary novel. We thought perhaps you'd say a few words just to set the ball rolling, and then answer questions.'

Martins at that moment was prepared to agree to anything to get rid of Mr Crabbin and also to secure a week's free board and lodging; and Rollo, of course, as I was to discover later, had always been prepared to accept any suggestion – for a drink, for a girl, for a joke, for a new excitement. He said now, 'Of course, of course,' into his handkerchief.

'Excuse me, Mr Dexter, have you got toothache? I know a very good dentist.'

'No. Somebody hit me, that's all.'

'Good God! Were they trying to rob you?'

'No, it was a soldier. I was trying to punch his bloody colonel in the eye.' He removed the handkerchief and gave Crabbin a view of his cut mouth. He told me that Crabbin was at a complete loss for words. Martins couldn't understand why because he had never read the work of his great contemporary, Benjamin Dexter: he hadn't even heard of him. I am a great admirer of Dexter, so that I could understand Crabbin's bewilderment. Dexter has been ranked as a stylist with Henry James, but he has a wider feminine streak than his master – indeed his enemies have sometimes described his subtle, complex, wavering style as old-maidish. For a man still just on the right side of fifty his passionate interest in embroidery and his habit of calming a not very tumultuous mind with tatting – a trait beloved by his disciples – certainly to others seems a little affected.

'Have you ever read a book called *The Lone Rider of Santa Fé*?'

'No, I don't think so.'

Martins said, 'This lone rider had his best friend shot by the sheriff of a town called Lost Claim Gulch. The story is how he hunted that sheriff down – quite legally – until his revenge was completed.'

'I never imagined you reading Westerns, Mr Dexter,' Crabbin said, and it needed all Martins' resolution to stop Rollo saying, 'But I write them.'

'Well, I'm gunning just the same way for Colonel Callaghan.'

'Never heard of him.'

'Heard of Harry Lime?'

'Yes,' Crabbin said cautiously, 'but I didn't really know him.'

'I did. He was my best friend.'

'I shouldn't have thought he was a very – literary character.'

'None of my friends are.'

Crabbin blinked nervously behind the horn-rims. He said with an air of appeasement, 'He was interested in the theatre though. A friend of his – an actress, you know – is learning English at the Institute. He called once or twice to fetch her.'

'Young or old?'

'Oh, young, very young. Not a good actress in my opinion.'

Martins remembered the girl by the grave with her hands over her face. He said, 'I'd like to meet any friend of Harry's.'

'She'll probably be at your lecture.'

'Austrian?'

'She claims to be Austrian, but I suspect she's Hungarian. She works at the Josefstadt.'

'Why claims to be Austrian?'

'The Russians sometimes get interested in the Hungarians. I wouldn't be surprised if Lime had helped her with her papers. She calls herself Schmidt. Anna Schmidt. You can't imagine a young English actress calling herself Smith, can you? And a pretty one, too. It always struck me as a bit too anonymous to be true.'

Martins felt he had got all he could from Crabbin, so he pleaded tiredness, a long day, promised to ring up in the morning, accepted ten pounds' worth of bafs for immediate expenses, and went to his room. It seemed to him that he was earning money rapidly – twelve pounds in less than an hour.

He *was* tired: he realized that when he stretched himself out on the bed in his boots. Within a minute he had left Vienna far behind him and was walking through a dense wood, ankle-deep in snow. An owl hooted, and he felt suddenly lonely and scared. He had an appointment to meet Harry under a particular tree, but in a wood so dense how could he recognize any one tree from

31

the rest? Then he saw a figure and ran towards it: it whistled a familiar tune and his heart lifted with relief and joy at not after all being alone. The figure turned and it was not Harry at all – just a stranger who grinned at him in a little circle of wet slushy melted snow, while the owl hooted again and again. He woke suddenly to hear the telephone ringing by his bed.

A voice with a trace of foreign accent – only a trace – said, 'Is that Mr Rollo Martins?'

'Yes.' It was a change to be himself and not Dexter.

'You wouldn't know me,' the voice said unnecessarily, 'but I was a friend of Harry Lime.'

It was a change too to hear anyone claim to be a friend of Harry's. Martins' heart warmed toward the stranger. He said, 'I'd be glad to meet you.'

'I'm just round the corner at the Old Vienna.'

'Couldn't you make it tomorrow? I've had a pretty awful day with one thing and another.'

'Harry asked me to see that you were all right. I was with him when he died.'

'I thought –' Rollo Martins said and stopped. He had been going to say, 'I thought he died instantaneously,' but something suggested caution. He said instead, 'You haven't told me your name.'

'Kurtz,' the voice said. 'I'd offer to come round to you, only, you know, Austrians aren't allowed in Sacher's.'

'Perhaps we could meet at the Old Vienna in the morning.'

'Certainly,' the voice said, 'if you are *quite* sure that you are all right till then?'

'How do you mean?'

'Harry had it on his mind that you'd be penniless.'

Rollo Martins lay back on his bed with the receiver to his ear and thought: Come to Vienna to make money. This was the third stranger to stake him in less than five hours. He said cautiously, 'Oh, I can carry on till I see you.' There seemed no point in turning down a good offer till he knew what the offer was.

'Shall we say eleven, then, at the Old Vienna in the Kärntnerstrasse ? I'll be in a brown suit and I'll carry one of your books.'

'That's fine. How did you get hold of one ?'

'Harry gave it to me.' The voice had enormous charm and reasonableness, but when Martins had said good night and rung off, he couldn't help wondering how it was that if Harry had been so conscious before he died he had not had a cable sent to stop him. Hadn't Callaghan too said that Lime died instantaneously – or without pain, was it ? – or had he put the words into Callaghan's mouth ? It was then the idea first lodged firmly in Martins' mind that there was something wrong about Lime's death, something the police had been too stupid to discover. He tried to discover it himself with the help of two cigarettes, but he fell asleep without his dinner and with the mystery still unsolved. It had been a long day, but not quite long enough for that.

[4]

'What I disliked about him at first sight,' Martins told me, 'was his toupée. It was one of those obvious toupées – flat and yellow, with the hair cut straight at the back and not fitting close. There *must* be something phoney about a man who won't accept baldness gracefully. He had one of those faces too where the lines have been put

33

in carefully, like a make-up, in the right places – to express charm, whimsicality, lines at the corners of the eyes. He was made up to appeal to romantic school-girls.'

This conversation took place some days later – he brought out his whole story when the trail was nearly cold. We were sitting in the Old Vienna at the table he had occupied that first morning with Kurtz, and when he made that remark about the romantic schoolgirls I saw his rather hunted eyes focus suddenly. It was a girl – just like any other girl, I thought, hurrying by outside in the driving snow.

'Something pretty?'

He brought his gaze back and said, 'I'm off that for ever. You know, Calloway, a time comes in a man's life when he gives up all that sort of thing . . .'

'I see. I thought you were looking at a girl.'

'I was. But only because she reminded me for a moment of Anna – Anna Schmidt.'

'Who's she? Isn't she a girl?'

'Oh, yes, in a way.'

'What do you mean, in a way?'

'She was Harry's girl.'

'Are you taking her over?'

'She's not that kind, Calloway. Didn't you see her at his funeral? I'm not mixing my drinks any more. I've got a hangover to last me a lifetime.'

'You were telling me about Kurtz,' I said.

It appeared that Kurtz was sitting there, making a great show of reading *The Lone Rider of Santa Fé*. When Martins sat down at his table he said with indescribably false enthusiasm, 'It's wonderful how you keep the tension.'

'Tension?'

'Suspense. You're a master at it. At the end of every chapter one's left guessing . . .'

'So you were a friend of Harry's,' Martins said.

'I think his best,' but Kurtz added with the smallest pause, in which his brain must have registered the error, 'except you, of course.'

'Tell me how he died.'

'I was with him. We came out together from the door of his flat and Harry saw a friend he knew across the road – an American called Cooler. He waved to Cooler and started across the road to him when a jeep came tearing round the corner and bowled him over. It was Harry's fault really – not the driver's.'

'Somebody told me he died instantaneously.'

'I wish he had. He died before the ambulance could reach us though.'

'He could speak, then?'

'Yes. Even in his pain he worried about you.'

'What did he say?'

'I can't remember the exact words, Rollo – I may call you Rollo, mayn't I? He always called you that to us. He was anxious that I should look after you when you arrived. See that you were looked after. Get your return ticket for you.' In telling me, Martins said, 'You see I was collecting return tickets as well as cash.'

'But why didn't you cable to stop me?'

'We did, but the cable must have missed you. What with censorship and the zones, cables can take anything up to five days.'

'There was an inquest?'

'Of course.'

'Did you know that the police have a crazy notion that Harry was mixed up in some racket?'

'No. But everyone in Vienna is. We all sell cigarettes and exchange schillings for bafs and that kind of thing. You won't find a single member of the Control Commission who hasn't broken the rules.'

'The police meant something worse than that.'

'They get rather absurd ideas sometimes,' the man with the toupée said cautiously.

'I'm going to stay here till I prove them wrong.'

Kurtz turned his head sharply and the toupée shifted very very slightly. He said, 'What's the good? Nothing can bring Harry back.'

'I'm going to have that police officer run out of Vienna.'

'I don't see what you can do.'

'I'm going to start working back from his death. You were there and this man Cooler and the chauffeur. You can give me their addresses.'

'I don't know the chauffeur's.'

'I can get it from the coroner's records. And then there's Harry's girl . . .'

Kurtz said, 'It will be painful for her.'

'I'm not concerned about her. I'm concerned about Harry.'

'Do you know what it is that the police suspect?'

'No. I lost my temper too soon.'

'Has it occurred to you,' Kurtz said gently, 'that you might dig up something – well, discreditable to Harry?'

'I'll risk that.'

'It will take a bit of time – and money.'

'I've got time and you were going to lend me some money, weren't you?'

'I'm not a rich man,' Kurtz said. 'I promised Harry to see you were all right and that you got your plane back . . .'

'You needn't worry about the money – or the plane,' Martins said. 'But I'll make a bet with you – in pounds sterling – five pounds against two hundred schillings – that there's something queer about Harry's death.'

It was a shot in the dark, but already he had this firm instinctive sense that there was something wrong, though he hadn't yet attached the word 'murder' to the instinct. Kurtz had a cup of coffee half-way to his lips and Martins watched him. The shot apparently went wide; an unaffected hand held the cup to the mouth and Kurtz drank, a little noisily, in long sips. Then he put down the cup and said, 'How do you mean – queer?'

'It was convenient for the police to have a corpse, but wouldn't it have been equally convenient, perhaps, for the real racketeers?' When he had spoken he realized that after all Kurtz might not have been unaffected by his wild statement: hadn't he perhaps been frozen into caution and calm? The hands of the guilty don't necessarily tremble; only in stories does a dropped glass betray agitation. Tension is more often shown in the studied action. Kurtz had drunk his coffee as though nothing had been said.

'Well –' he took another sip – 'of course I wish you luck, though I don't believe there's anything to find. Just ask me for any help you want.'

'I want Cooler's address.'

'Certainly. I'll write it down for you. Here it is. In the American zone.'

'And yours?'

'I've already put it – underneath. I'm unlucky enough to be in the Russian zone – so don't visit me very late.

Things sometimes happen round our way.' He was giving one of his studied Viennese smiles, the charm carefully painted in with a fine brush in the little lines about the mouth and eyes. 'Keep in touch,' he said, 'and if you need any help . . . but I still think you are very unwise.' He touched *The Lone Rider*. 'I'm so proud to have met you. A master of suspense,' and one hand smoothed the toupée, while another, passing softly over the mouth, brushed out the smile as though it had never been.

[5]

Martins sat on a hard chair just inside the stage door of the Josefstadt Theatre. He had sent up his card to Anna Schmidt after the matinée, marking it 'a friend of Harry's'. An arcade of little windows, with lace curtains and the lights going out one after another, showed where the artists were packing up for home, for the cup of coffee without sugar, the roll without butter to sustain them for the evening performance. It was like a little street built indoors for a film set, but even indoors it was cold, even cold to a man in a heavy overcoat, so that Martins rose and walked up and down underneath the little windows. He felt, he said, rather like a Romeo who wasn't sure of Juliet's balcony.

He had had time to think: he was calm now, Martins not Rollo was in the ascendant. When a light went out in one of the windows and an actress descended into the passage where he walked, he didn't even turn to take a look. He was done with all that. He thought, Kurtz is right. They are all right. I'm behaving like a romantic fool. I'll just have a word with Anna Schmidt, a word of commiseration, and then I'll pack and go. He had quite forgotten, he told me, the complication of Mr Crabbin.

A voice over his head called 'Mr Martins,' and he looked up at the face that watched him from between the curtains a few feet above his head. It wasn't a beautiful face, he firmly explained to me, when I accused him of once again mixing his drinks. Just an honest face; dark hair and eyes which in that light looked brown; a wide forehead, a large mouth which didn't try to charm. No danger anywhere, it seemed to Rollo Martins, of that sudden reckless moment when the scent of hair or a hand against the side alters life. She said, 'Will you come up, please? The second door on the right.'

There are some people, he explained to me carefully, whom one recognizes instantaneously as friends. You can be at ease with them because you know that never, never will you be in danger. 'That was Anna,' he said, and I wasn't sure whether the past tense was deliberate or not.

Unlike most actresses' rooms this one was almost bare; no wardrobe packed with clothes, no clutter of cosmetics and grease-paints; a dressing-gown on the door, one sweater he recognized from Act II on the only easy chair, a tin of half-used paints and grease. A kettle hummed softly on a gas ring. She said, 'Would you like a cup of tea? Someone sent me a packet last week – sometimes the Americans do, instead of flowers, you know, on the first night.'

'I'd like a cup,' he said, but if there was one thing he hated it was tea. He watched her while she made it, made it, of course, all wrong: the water not on the boil, the teapot unheated, too few leaves. She said, 'I never quite understand why English people like tea.'

He drank his cupful quickly like a medicine and

watched her gingerly and delicately sip at hers. He said, 'I wanted very much to see you. About Harry.'

It was the dreadful moment; he could see her mouth stiffen to meet it.

'Yes?'

'I had known him twenty years. I was his friend. We were at school together, you know, and after that – there weren't many months running when we didn't meet . . .'

She said, 'When I got your card, I couldn't say no. But there's nothing really for us to talk about, is there? – nothing.'

'I wanted to hear ——'

'He's dead. That's the end. Everything's over, finished. What's the good of talking?'

'We both loved him.'

'I don't know. You can't know a thing like that – afterwards. I don't know anything any more except——'

'Except?'

'That I want to be dead too.'

Martins told me, 'Then I nearly went away. What was the good of tormenting her because of this wild idea of mine? But instead I asked her one question. "Do you know a man called Cooler?"'

'An American?' she asked. 'I think that was the man who brought me some money when Harry died. I didn't want to take it, but he said Harry had been anxious – at the last moment.'

'So he didn't die instantaneously?'

'Oh, no.'

Martins said to me, 'I began to wonder why I had got that idea so firmly into my head, and then I thought it was only the man in the flat who told me so – no one else. I said to her, "He must have been very clear in his head at the end – because he remembered about me too. That seems to show that there wasn't really any pain."'

'That's what I tell myself all the time.'

'Did you see the doctor?'

'Once. Harry sent me to him. He was Harry's own doctor. He lived near by, you see.'

Martins suddenly saw in that odd chamber of the mind that constructs such pictures, instantaneously, irrationally, a desert place, a body on the ground, a group of birds gathered. Perhaps it was a scene from one of his own books, not yet written, forming at the gate of consciousness. It faded, and he thought how odd that they were all there, just at that moment, all Harry's friends – Kurtz, the doctor, this man Cooler; only the two people who loved him seemed to have been missing. He said, 'And the driver? Did you hear his evidence?'

'He was upset, scared. But Cooler's evidence exonerated him. No, it wasn't his fault, poor man. I've often heard Harry say what a careful driver he was.'

'He knew Harry too?' Another bird flapped down and joined the others round the silent figure on the sand who lay face down. Now he could tell that it was Harry, by the clothes, by the attitude like that of a boy asleep in the grass at a playing-field's edge, on a hot summer afternoon.

Somebody called outside the window, 'Fräulein Schmidt.'

She said, 'They don't like one to stay too long. It uses up *their* electricity.'

He had given up the idea of sparing her anything. He told her, 'The police say they were going to arrest Harry. They'd pinned some racket on him.'

She took the news in much the same way as Kurtz. 'Everybody's in a racket.'

'I don't believe he was in anything serious.'

'No.'

'But he may have been framed. Do you know a man named Kurtz?'

'I don't think so.'

'He wears a toupée.'

'Oh.' He could tell that that struck home. He said, 'Don't you think that it was odd they were all there – at the death? Everybody knew Harry. Even the driver, the doctor . . .'

She said with hopeless calm, 'I've wondered that too, though I didn't know about Kurtz. I wondered whether they'd murdered him, but what's the use of wondering?'

'I'm going to get those bastards,' Rollo Martins said.

'It won't do any good. Perhaps the police are right. Perhaps poor Harry got mixed up——'

'Fräulein Schmidt,' the voice called again.

'I must go.'

'I'll walk with you a bit of the way.'

The dark was almost down; the snow had ceased for a while to fall, and the great statues of the Ring, the prancing horses, the chariots and eagles, were gun-shot grey with the end of evening. 'It's better to give up and forget,' Anna said. The moon-lit snow lay ankle-deep on the unswept pavements.

'Will you give me the doctor's address?'

They stood in the shelter of a wall while she wrote it down for him.

'And yours too?'

'Why do you want that?'

'I might have news for you.'

'There isn't any news that would do any good now.'

He watched her from a distance board her tram, bowing

42

her head against the wind, a dark question mark on the snow.

[6]

An amateur detective has this advantage over the professional, that he doesn't work set hours. Rollo Martins was not confined to the eight-hour day: his investigations didn't have to pause for meals. In his one day he covered as much ground as one of my men would have covered in two, and he had this initial advantage over us, that he was Harry's friend. He was, as it were, working from inside, while we pecked at the perimeter.

Dr Winkler was at home. Perhaps he would not have been at home to a police officer. Again Martins had marked his card with the open-sesame phrase: 'A friend of Harry Lime's.'

Dr Winkler's waiting-room reminded Martins of an antique shop – an antique shop that specializes in religious *objets d'art*. There were more crucifixes than he could count, none of later date probably than the seventeenth century. There were statues in wood and ivory. There were a number of reliquaries: little bits of bone marked with saints' names and set in oval frames on a background of tinfoil. If they were genuine, what an odd fate it was, Martins thought, for a portion of Saint Susanna's knuckle to come to rest in Dr Winkler's waiting-room. Even the high-backed hideous chairs looked as if they had once been sat in by cardinals. The room was stuffy, and one expected the smell of incense. In a small gold casket was a splinter of the True Cross. A sneeze disturbed him.

Dr Winkler was the cleanest doctor Martins had ever

seen. He was very small and neat, in a black tail-coat and a high stiff collar; his little black moustache was like an evening tie. He sneezed again: perhaps he was cold because he was so clean. He said, 'Mr Martins?'

An irresistible desire to sully Dr Winkler assailed Rollo Martins. He said, 'Dr Winkle?'

'Dr Winkler.'

'You've got an interesting collection here.'

'Yes.'

'These saints' bones . . .'

'The bones of chickens and rabbits.' Dr Winkler took a large white handkerchief out of his sleeve rather as though he were a conjurer producing his country's flag, and blew his nose neatly and thoroughly twice, closing each nostril in turn. You expected him to throw away the handkerchief after one use. 'Would you mind, Mr Martins, telling me the purpose of your visit? I have a patient waiting.'

'We were both friends of Harry Lime.'

'I was his medical adviser,' Dr Winkler corrected him and waited obstinately between the crucifixes.

'I arrived too late for the inquest. Harry had invited me out here to help him in something. I don't quite know what. I didn't hear of his death till I arrived.'

'Very sad,' Dr Winkler said.

'Naturally, under the circumstances, I want to hear all I can.'

'There is nothing I can tell you that you don't know. He was knocked over by a car. He was dead when I arrived.'

'Would he have been conscious at all?'

'I understand he was for a short time, while they carried him into the house.'

44

'In great pain?'

'Not necessarily.'

'You are quite certain that it was an accident?'

Dr Winkler put out a hand and straightened a crucifix. 'I was not there. My opinion is limited to the cause of death. Have you any reason to be dissatisfied?'

The amateur has another advantage over the professional: he can be reckless. He can tell unnecessary truths and propound wild theories. Martins said, 'The police have implicated Harry in a very serious racket. It seemed to me that he might have been murdered – or even killed himself.'

'I am not competent to pass an opinion,' Dr Winkler said.

'Do you know a man called Cooler?'

'I don't think so.'

'He was there when Harry was killed.'

'Then of course I have met him. He wears a toupée.'

'That was Kurtz.'

Dr Winkler was not only the cleanest, he was also the most cautious doctor that Martins had ever met. His statements were so limited that you could not for a moment doubt their veracity. He said, 'There was a second man there.' If he had to diagnose a case of scarlet fever he would, you felt, have confined himself to a statement that a rash was visible, that the temperature was so and so. He would never find himself in error at an inquest.

'Had you been Harry's doctor for long?' He seemed an odd man for Harry to choose – Harry who liked men with a certain recklessness, men capable of making mistakes.

'For about a year.'

'Well, it's good of you to have seen me.' Dr Winkler bowed. When he bowed there was a very slight creak as though his shirt were made of celluloid. 'I mustn't keep you from your patients any longer.' Turning away from Dr Winkler, he confronted yet another crucifix, the figure hanging with arms above the head: a face of elongated El Greco agony. 'That's a strange crucifix,' he said.

'Jansenist,' Dr Winkler commented and closed his mouth sharply as though he had been guilty of giving away too much information.

'Never heard the word. Why are the arms above the head?'

Dr Winkler said reluctantly, 'Because He died, in their view, only for the elect.'

[7]

As I see it, turning over my files, the notes of conversations, the statements of various characters, it would have been still possible, at this moment, for Rollo Martins to have left Vienna safely. He had shown an unhealthy curiosity, but the disease had been checked at every point. Nobody had given anything away. The smooth wall of deception had as yet shown no real crack to his roaming fingers. When Rollo Martins left Dr Winkler's he was in no danger. He could have gone home to bed at Sacher's and slept with a quiet mind. He could even have visited Cooler at this stage without trouble. No one was seriously disturbed. Unfortunately for him – and there would always be periods of his life when he bitterly regretted it – he chose to go back to Harry's flat. He wanted to talk to the little vexed man who said he had seen the accident – or had he really not said so much? There was a moment in the dark frozen street when he was inclined to go straight to Cooler, to complete his picture of those sinister birds who sat around Harry's body, but Rollo, being Rollo, decided to toss a coin and the coin fell for the other action, and the deaths of two men.

Perhaps the little man – who bore the name of Koch – had drunk a glass too much of wine, perhaps he had simply spent a good day at the office, but this time, when Rollo Martins rang his bell, he was friendly and quite ready to talk. He had just finished dinner and had crumbs on his moustache. 'Ah, I remember you. You are Herr Lime's friend.'

He welcomed Martins in with great cordiality and introduced him to a mountainous wife whom he obviously kept under very strict control. 'Ah, in the old days, I would have offered you a cup of coffee, but now——'

Martins passed round his cigarette case and the atmosphere of cordiality deepened. 'When you came yesterday I was a little abrupt,' Herr Koch said, 'but I had a touch of migraine and my wife was out, so I had to answer the door myself.'

'Did you tell me that you had actually seen the accident?'

Herr Koch exchanged glances with his wife. 'The inquest is over, Ilse. There is no harm. You can trust my judgement. The gentleman is a friend. Yes, I saw the accident, but you are the only one who knows. When I say that I saw it, perhaps I should say that I heard it. I heard the brakes put on and the sound of the skid, and I got to the window in time to see them carry the body to the house.'

'But didn't you give evidence?'

47

'It is better not to be mixed up in such things. My office cannot spare me. We are short of staff, and of course I did not actually *see*——'

'But you told me yesterday how it happened.'

'That was how they described it in the papers.'

'Was he in great pain?'

'He was dead. I looked right down from my window here and I saw his face. I know when a man is dead. You see, it is, in a way, my business. I am the head clerk at the mortuary.'

'But the others say that he did not die at once.'

'Perhaps they don't know death as well as I do.'

'He was dead, of course, when the doctor arrived. He told me that.'

'He was dead at once. You can take the word of a man who knows.'

'I think, Herr Koch, that you should have given evidence.'

'One must look after oneself, Herr Martins. I was not the only one who should have been there.'

'How do you mean?'

'There were three people who helped to carry your friend to the house.'

'I know – two men and the driver.'

'The driver stayed where he was. He was very much shaken, poor man.'

'Three men . . .' It was as though suddenly, fingering that bare wall, his fingers had encountered, not so much a crack perhaps, but at least a roughness that had not been smoothed away by the careful builders.

'Can you describe the men?'

But Herr Koch was not trained to observe the living: only the man with the toupée had attracted his eyes – the

48

other two were just men, neither tall nor short, thick nor thin. He had seen them from far above, foreshortened, bent over their burden; they had not looked up, and he had quickly looked away and closed the window, realizing at once the wisdom of not being seen himself.

'There was no evidence I could really give, Herr Martins.'

No evidence, Martins thought, no evidence! He no longer doubted that murder had been done. Why else had they lied about the moment of death? They wanted to quieten with their gifts of money and their plane ticket the only two friends Harry had in Vienna. And the third man? Who was he?

He said, 'Did you see Herr Lime go out?'

'No.'

'Did you hear a scream?'

'Only the brakes, Herr Martins.'

It occurred to Martins that there was nothing – except the word of Kurtz and Cooler and the driver – to prove that in fact Harry had been killed at that precise moment. There was the medical evidence, but that could not prove more than that he had died, say, within a half-hour, and in any case the medical evidence was only as strong as Dr Winkler's word: that clean controlled man creaking among his crucifixes.

'Herr Martins, it just occurs to me – you are staying in Vienna?'

'Yes.'

'If you need accommodation and spoke to the authorities quickly, you might secure Herr Lime's flat. It is a requisitioned property.'

'Who has the keys?'

'I have them.'

49

'Could I see the flat?'

'Ilse, the keys.'

Herr Koch led the way into the flat that had been Harry's. In the little dark hall there was still the smell of cigarette smoke – the Turkish cigarettes that Harry always smoked. It seemed odd that a man's smell should cling in the folds of a curtain so long after the man himself had become dead matter, a gas, a decay. One light, in a heavily beaded shade, left them in semi-darkness, fumbling for door handles.

The living-room was completely bare – it seemed to Martins too bare. The chairs had been pushed up against the walls; the desk at which Harry must have written was free from dust or any papers. The parquet reflected the light like a mirror. Herr Koch opened a door and showed the bedroom: the bed neatly made with clean sheets. In the bathroom not even a used razor blade indicated that a few days ago a living man had occupied it. Only the dark hall and the cigarette smell gave a sense of occupation.

'You see,' Herr Koch said, 'it is quite ready for a new-comer. Ilse has cleaned up.'

That she certainly had done. After a death there should have been more litter left than this. A man can't go suddenly and unexpectedly on his longest journey without forgetting this or that, without leaving a bill un-paid, an official form unanswered, the photograph of a girl. 'Were there no papers, Herr Koch?'

'Herr Lime was always a very tidy man. His waste-paper basket was full and his brief-case, but his friend fetched that away.'

'His friend?'

'The gentleman with the toupée.'

It was possible, of course, that Lime had not taken the journey so unexpectedly, and it occurred to Martins that Lime had perhaps hoped he would arrive in time to help. He said to Herr Koch, 'I believe my friend was murdered.'

'Murdered?' Herr Koch's cordiality was snuffed out by the word. He said, 'I would not have asked you in here if I had thought you would talk such nonsense.'

'Why should it be nonsense?'

'We do not have murders in this zone.'

'All the same, your evidence may be very valuable.'

'I have no evidence. I saw nothing. I am not concerned. You must leave here at once, please. You have been very inconsiderate.' He hustled Martins back through the hall; already the smell of the smoke was fading a little more. Herr Koch's last words before he slammed his own door was, 'It's no concern of mine.' Poor Herr Koch! We do not choose our concerns. Later, when I was questioning Martins closely, I said to him, 'Did you see anybody at all on the stairs, or in the street outside?'

'Nobody.' He had everything to gain by remembering some chance passer-by, and I believed him. He said, 'I noticed myself how quiet and dead the whole street looked. Part of it had been bombed, you know, and the moon was shining on the snow slopes. It was so very silent. I could hear my own feet creaking in the snow.'

'Of course, it proves nothing. There is a basement where anybody who had followed you could have hidden.'

'Yes.'

'Or your whole story may be phoney.'

'Yes.'

'The trouble is I can see no motive for you to have done it. It's true you are already guilty of getting money on false pretences. You came out here to join Lime, perhaps to help him . . .'

Martins said to me, 'What was this precious racket you keep on hinting at?'

'I'd have told you all the facts when I first saw you if you hadn't lost your temper so damned quickly. Now I don't think I shall be acting wisely to tell you. It would be disclosing official information, and your contacts, you know, don't inspire confidence. A girl with phoney papers supplied by Lime, this man Kurtz . . .'

'Dr Winkler . . .'

'I've got nothing against Dr Winkler. No, if you are phoney, you don't need the information, but it might help you to learn exactly what we know. You see, our facts are not complete.'

'I bet they aren't. I could invent a better detective than you in my bath.'

'Your literary style does not do your namesake justice.' Whenever he was reminded of Mr Crabbin, that poor harassed representative of the British Council, Rollo Martins turned pink, with annoyance, embarrassment, shame. That too inclined me to trust him.

He had certainly given Crabbin some uncomfortable hours. On returning to Sacher's Hotel after his interview with Herr Koch he had found a desperate note waiting for him from the representative.

'I have been trying to locate you all day,' Crabbin wrote. 'It is essential that we should get together and work out a proper programme for you. This morning by telephone I have arranged lectures at Innsbruck and Salzburg for next week, but I must have your consent to

52

the subjects, so that proper programmes can be printed. I would suggest two lectures: "The Crisis of Faith in the Western World" (you are very respected here as a Christian writer, but this lecture should be quite un-political and no references should be made to Russia or Communism) and "The Technique of the Contemporary Novel". The same lectures would be given in Vienna. Apart from this, there are a great many people here who would like to meet you, and I want to arrange a cocktail party for early next week. But for all this I must have a few words with you.' The letter ended on a note of acute anxiety. 'You will be at the discussion tomorrow night, won't you? We all expect you at 8.30 and, need-less to say, look forward to your coming. I will send transport to the hotel at 8.15 sharp.'

Rollo Martins read the letter and, without bothering any further about Mr Crabbin, went to bed.

[8]

After two drinks Rollo Martins' mind would always turn towards women – in a vague, sentimental, romantic way, as a sex, in general. After three drinks, like a pilot who dives to find direction, he would begin to focus on one available girl. If he had not been offered a third drink by Cooler, he would probably not have gone quite so soon to Anna Schmidt's house, and if – but there are too many 'ifs' in my style of writing, for it is my pro-fession to balance possibilities, human possibilities, and the drive of destiny can never find a place in my files.

Martins had spent his lunch-time reading up the reports of the inquest, thus again demonstrating the superiority of the amateur to the professional, and making him more vulnerable to Cooler's liquor (which the professional in duty bound would have refused). It was nearly five o'clock when he reached Cooler's flat, which was over an ice-cream parlour in the American zone: the bar below was full of G.I.s with their girls, and the clatter of the long spoons and the curious free unformed laughter followed him up the stairs.

The Englishman who objects to Americans in general usually carries in his mind's eye just such an exception as Cooler: a man with tousled grey hair and a worried kindly face and long-sighted eyes, the kind of humanitarian who turns up in a typhus epidemic or a world war or a Chinese famine long before his countrymen have discovered the place in an atlas. Again the card marked 'Harry's friend' was like an entrance ticket. Cooler was in officer's uniform, with mysterious letters on his flash, and no badges of rank, although his maid referred to him as Colonel Cooler. His warm frank handclasp was the most friendly act that Martins had encountered in Vienna.

'Any friend of Harry is all right with me,' Cooler said. 'I've heard of you, of course.'

'From Harry?'

'I'm a great reader of Westerns,' Cooler said, and Martins believed him as he did not believe Kurtz.

'I wondered – you were there, weren't you? – if you'd tell me about Harry's death.'

'It was a terrible thing,' Cooler said. 'I was just crossing the road to go to Harry. He and Mr Kurtz were on the sidewalk. Maybe if I hadn't started across the road, he'd have stayed where he was. But he saw me and stepped straight off to meet me and this jeep – it was terrible, terrible. The driver braked, but he didn't stand a chance. Have a Scotch, Mr Martins. It's silly of me, but I get shaken up when I think of it.' He said as he splashed in the soda, 'In spite of this uniform, I'd never seen a man killed before.'

'Was the other man in the car?'

Cooler took a long pull and then measured what was left with his tired kindly eyes. 'What man would you be referring to, Mr Martins?'

'I was told there was another man there.'

'I don't know how you got that idea. You'll find all about it in the inquest reports.' He poured out two more generous drinks. 'There were just the three of us – me and Mr Kurtz and the driver. The doctor, of course. I expect you were thinking of the doctor.'

'This man I was talking to happened to look out of a window – he has the next flat to Harry's – and he said he saw three men and the driver. That's before the doctor arrived.'

'He didn't say that in court.'

'He didn't want to get involved.'

'You'll never teach these Europeans to be good citizens. It was his duty.' Cooler brooded sadly over his glass. 'It's an odd thing, Mr Martins, with accidents. You'll never get two reports that coincide. Why, even Mr Kurtz and I disagreed about details. The thing happens so suddenly, you aren't concerned to notice things, until bang crash, and then you have to reconstruct, remember. I expect he got too tangled up trying to sort out what happened before and what after, to distinguish the four of us.'

'The four?'

'I was counting Harry. What else did he see, Mr Martins?'

'Nothing of interest – except he says Harry was dead when he was carried to the house.'

'Well, he was dying – not much difference there. Have another drink, Mr Martins?'

'No, I don't think I will.'

'Well, I'd like another spot. I was very fond of your friend, Mr Martins, and I don't like talking about it.'

'Perhaps one more – to keep you company. Do you know Anna Schmidt?' Martins asked, while the whisky tingled on his tongue.

'Harry's girl? I met her once, that's all. As a matter of fact, I helped Harry fix her papers. Not the sort of thing I should confess to a stranger, I suppose, but you have to break the rules sometimes. Humanity's a duty too.'

'What was wrong?'

'She was Hungarian and her father had been a Nazi, so they said. She was scared the Russians would pick her up.'

'Why should they want to?'

'We can't always figure out why they do these things. Perhaps just to show that it's not healthy being friends with an Englishman.'

'But she lives in the British zone.'

'That wouldn't stop them. It's only five minutes' ride in a jeep from the Commandatura. The streets aren't well lighted, and you haven't many police around.'

'You took her some money from Harry, didn't you?'

'Yes, but I wouldn't have mentioned that. Did she tell you?'

The telephone rang, and Cooler drained his glass. 'Hullo,' he said. 'Why, yes. This is Colonel Cooler.' Then he sat with the receiver at his ear and an expression of sad patience, while some voice a long way off drained into the room. 'Yes,' he said once. 'Yes.' His eyes dwelt on Martins' face, but they seemed to be looking a long way beyond him: flat and tired and kind, they might have been gazing out across the sea. He said, 'You did quite right,' in a tone of commendation, and then, with a touch of asperity, 'Of course they will be delivered. I gave my word. Good-bye.'

He put the receiver down and passed a hand across his forehead wearily. It was as though he were trying to remember something he had to do. Martins said, 'Had you heard anything of this racket the police talk about?'

'I'm sorry. What's that?'

'They say Harry was mixed up in some racket.'

'Oh, no,' Cooler said. 'No. That's quite impossible. He had a great sense of duty.'

'Kurtz seemed to think it was possible.'

'Kurtz doesn't understand how an Anglo-Saxon feels,' Cooler replied.

[9]

It was nearly dark when Martins made his way along the banks of the canal: across the water lay the half-destroyed Diana baths and in the distance the great black circle of the Prater Wheel, stationary above the ruined houses. Over there across the grey water was the Second Bezirk, in Russian ownership. St Stephanskirche shot its enormous wounded spire into the sky above the Inner City, and, coming up the Kärntnerstrasse, Martins passed the lit door of the Military Police station. The four men of the International Patrol were climbing into their jeep; the Russian M.P. sat beside the driver (for the Russians had that day taken over the chair for the next four weeks)

57

and the Englishman, the Frenchman, and the American mounted behind. The third stiff whisky fumed into Martins' brain, and he remembered the girl in Amsterdam, the girl in Paris; loneliness moved along the crowded pavement at his side. He passed the corner of the street where Sacher's lay and went on. Rollo was in control and moved towards the only girl he knew in Vienna.

I asked him how he knew where she lived. Oh, he said, he'd looked up the address she had given him the night before, in bed, studying a map. He wanted to know his way about, and he was good with maps. He could memorize turnings and street names easily because he always went one way on foot.

'One way?'

'I mean when I'm calling on a girl – or someone.'

He hadn't, of course, known that she would be in, that her play was not on that night in the Josefstadt, or perhaps he had memorized that too from the posters. In at any rate she was, if you could really call it being in, sitting alone in an unheated room, with the bed disguised as a divan, and a typewritten script lying open at the first page on the inadequate too-fancy topply table – because her thoughts were so far from being 'in'. He said awkwardly (and nobody could have said, not even Rollo, how much his awkwardness was part of his technique), 'I thought I'd just look in and look you up. You see, I was passing . . .'

'Passing? Where to?' It had been a good half an hour's walk from the Inner City to the rim of the English zone, but he always had a reply. 'I had too much whisky with Colonel Cooler. I needed a walk and I just happened to find myself this way.'

'I can't give you a drink here. Except tea. There's some of that packet left.'

'No, no thank you.' He said, 'You are busy,' looking at the script.

'I didn't get beyond the first line.'

He picked it up and read: '*Enter Louise.* LOUISE: I heard a child crying.'

'Can I stay a little?' he asked with a gentleness that was more Martins than Rollo.

'I wish you would.' He slumped down on the divan, and he told me a long time later (for lovers reconstruct the smallest details if they can find a listener) that then it was he took his second real look at her. She stood there as awkward as himself in a pair of old flannel trousers which had been patched badly in the seat; she stood with her legs firmly straddled as though she were opposing someone and was determined to hold her ground – a small rather stocky figure with any grace she had folded and put away for use professionally.

'One of those bad days?' he asked.

'It's always bad about this time.' She explained, 'He used to look in, and when I heard you ring, just for a moment, I thought . . .' She sat down on a hard chair opposite him and said, 'Please talk. You knew him. Just tell me anything.'

And so he talked. The sky blackened outside the window while he talked. He noticed after a while that their hands had met. He said to me, 'I never meant to fall in love, not with Harry's girl.'

'When did it happen?' I asked him.

'It was very cold and I got up to close the window curtains. I only noticed my hand was on hers when I took it away. As I stood up I looked down at her face and she

59

was looking up. It wasn't a beautiful face – that was the trouble. It was a face to live with, day in, day out. A face for wear. I felt as though I'd come into a new country where I couldn't speak the language. I had always thought it was beauty one loved in a woman. I stood there at the curtains, waiting to pull them, looking out. I couldn't see anything but my own face, looking back into the room, looking for her. She said, "And what did Harry do that time?" and I wanted to say, "Damn Harry. He's dead. We both loved him, but he's dead. The dead are made to be forgotten." Instead, of course, all I said was, "What do you think? He just whistled his old tune as if nothing was the matter," and I whistled it to her as well as I could. I heard her catch her breath, and I looked round and before I could think: Is this the right way, the right card, the right gambit? – I'd already said, "He's dead. You can't go on remembering him for ever."'

She said, 'I know, but perhaps something will happen first.'

'What do you mean – something happen?'

'Oh, I mean perhaps there'll be another war, or I'll die, or the Russians will take me.'

'You'll forget him in time. You'll fall in love again.'

'I know, but I don't want to. Don't you see I don't want to?'

So Rollo Martins came back from the window and sat down on the divan again. When he had risen half a minute before he had been the friend of Harry, comforting Harry's girl; now he was a man in love with Anna Schmidt who had been in love with a man they had both once known called Harry Lime. He didn't speak again that evening about the past. Instead he began to tell her of the people he had seen. 'I can believe anything of Winkler,' he told her, 'but Cooler – I liked Cooler. He was the only one of his friends who stood up for Harry. The trouble is, if Cooler's right, then Koch is wrong, and I really thought I had something there.'

'Who's Koch?'

He explained how he had returned to Harry's flat and he described his interview with Koch, the story of the third man.

'If it's true,' she said, 'it's very important.'

'It doesn't prove anything. After all, Koch backed out of the inquest; so might this stranger.'

'That's not the point,' she said. 'It means that *they* lied: Kurtz and Cooler.'

'They might have lied so as not to inconvenience this fellow – if he was a friend.'

'Yet another friend – on the spot. And where's your Cooler's honesty then?'

'What do we do? Koch clamped down like an oyster and turned me out of his flat.'

'He won't turn me out,' she said, 'or his Ilse won't.'

They walked up the long road to the flat together; the snow clogged on their shoes and made them move slowly like convicts weighed down by irons. Anna Schmidt said, 'Is it far?'

'Not very far now. Do you see that knot of people up the road? It's somewhere about there.' The group was like a splash of ink on the whiteness, a splash that flowed, changed shape, spread out. When they came a little nearer Martins said, 'I think that's his block. What do you suppose this is, a political demonstration?'

Anna Schmidt stopped. She said, 'Who else have you told about Koch?'

'Only you and Colonel Cooler. Why?'

'I'm frightened. It reminds me . . .' She had her eyes fixed on the crowd and he never knew what memory out of her confused past had risen to warn her. 'Let's go away,' she implored him.

'You're crazy. We're on to something here, something big . . .'

'I'll wait for you.'

'But you're going to talk to him.'

'Find out first what all those people . . .' She said, strangely for one who worked behind the footlights, 'I hate crowds.'

He walked slowly on alone, the snow caking on his heels. It wasn't a political meeting, for no one was making a speech. He had the impression of heads turning to watch him come, as though he were somebody who was expected. When he reached the fringe of the little crowd, he knew for certain that it was the house. A man looked hard at him and said, 'Are you another of them?'

'What do you mean?'

'The police.'

'No. What are they doing?'

'They've been in and out all day.'

'What's everybody waiting for?'

'They want to see him brought out.'

'Who?'

'Herr Koch.' It occurred to Martins that somebody besides himself had discovered Herr Koch's failure to give evidence, though that was hardly a police matter. He said, 'What's he done?'

'Nobody knows that yet. They can't make their minds up in there – it might be suicide, you see, and it might be murder.'

'Herr Koch?'

'Of course.'

A small child came up to his informant and pulled at his hand. 'Papa, Papa.' He wore a wool cap on his head, like a gnome; his face was pinched and blue with cold.

'Yes, my dear, what is it?'

'I heard them talking through the grating, Papa.'

'Oh, you cunning little one. Tell us what you heard, Hansel.'

'I heard Frau Koch crying, Papa.'

'Was that all, Hansel?'

'No. I heard the big man talking, Papa.'

'Ah, you cunning little Hansel. Tell Papa what he said.'

'He said, "Can you tell me, Frau Koch, what the foreigner looked like?"'

'Ha, ha, you see, they think it's murder. And who's to say they are wrong? Why should Herr Koch cut his own throat in the basement?'

'Papa, Papa.'

'Yes, little Hansel?'

'When I looked through the grating, I could see some blood on the coke.'

'What a child you are. How could you tell it was blood? The snow leaks everywhere.' The man turned to Martins and said, 'The child has such an imagination. Maybe he will be a writer when he grows up.'

The pinched face stared solemnly up at Martins. The child said, 'Papa.'

'Yes, Hansel?'

'He's a foreigner too.'

The man gave a big laugh that caused a dozen heads to

turn. 'Listen to him, sir, listen,' he said proudly. 'He thinks you did it just because you are a foreigner. As though there weren't more foreigners here these days than Viennese.'

'Papa, Papa.'

'Yes, Hansel?'

'They are coming out.'

A knot of police surrounded the covered stretcher which they lowered carefully down the steps for fear of sliding on the trodden snow. The man said, 'They can't get an ambulance into this street because of the ruins. They have to carry it round the corner.' Frau Koch came out at the tail of the procession; she had a shawl over her head and an old sackcloth coat. Her thick shape looked like a snowman as she sank in a drift at the pavement's edge. Someone gave her a hand and she looked round with a lost hopeless gaze at this crowd of strangers. If there were friends there she did not recognize them, looking from face to face. Martins bent as she passed, fumbling at his shoelace, but looking up from the ground he saw at his own eyes' level the scrutinizing cold-blooded gnome-gaze of little Hansel.

Walking back down the street towards Anna, he looked back once. The child was pulling at his father's hand and he could see the lips forming round those syllables like the refrain of a grim ballad, 'Papa, Papa.'

He said to Anna, 'Koch has been murdered. Come away from here.' He walked as rapidly as the snow would let him, turning this corner and that. The child's suspicion and alertness seemed to spread like a cloud over the city – they could not walk fast enough to evade its shadow. He paid no attention when Anna said to him, 'Then what Koch said was true. There *was* a third man,'

64

nor a little later when she said, 'It must have been murder. You don't kill a man to hide anything less.'

The tramcars flashed like icicles at the end of the street: they were back at the Ring. Martins said, 'You had better go home alone. I'll keep away from you awhile till things have sorted out.'

'But nobody can suspect you.'

'They are asking about the foreigner who called on Koch yesterday. There may be some unpleasantness for a while.'

'Why don't you go to the police?'

'They are so stupid. I don't trust them. See what they've pinned on Harry. And then I tried to hit this man Callaghan. They'll have it in for me. The least they'll do is send me away from Vienna. But if I stay quiet – there's only one person who can give me away. Cooler.'

'And he won't want to.'

'Not if he's guilty. But then I can't believe he's guilty.'

Before she left him, she said, 'Be careful. Koch knew so very little and they murdered him. You know as much as Koch.'

The warning stayed in his brain all the way to Sacher's: after nine o'clock the streets are very empty, and he would turn his head at every padding step coming up the street behind him, as though that third man whom they had protected so ruthlessly were following him like an executioner. The Russian sentry outside the Grand Hotel looked rigid with the cold, but he was human, he had a face, an honest peasant face with Mongol eyes. The third man had no face: only the top of a head seen from a window. At Sacher's Mr Schmidt said, 'Colonel

Calloway has been in, asking for you, sir. I think you'll find him in the bar.'

'Back in a moment,' Martins said and walked straight out of the hotel again: he wanted time to think. But immediately he stepped outside a man came forward, touched his cap, and said firmly, 'Please, sir.' He flung open the door of a khaki-painted truck with a Union Jack on the windscreen and firmly urged Martins within. He surrendered without protest; sooner or later, he felt sure, inquiries would be made; he had only pretended optimism to Anna Schmidt.

The driver drove too fast for safety on the frozen road, and Martins protested. All he got in reply was a sullen grunt and a muttered sentence containing the word 'orders'. 'Have you orders to kill me?' Martins asked facetiously and got no reply at all. He caught sight of the Titans on the Hofburg balancing great globes of snow above their heads, and then they plunged into ill-lit streets beyond, where he lost all sense of direction.

'Is it far?' But the driver paid no attention at all. At least, Martins thought, I am not under arrest: they have not sent a guard; I am being invited – wasn't that the word they used? – to visit the station to make a statement.

The car drew up and the driver led the way up two flights of stairs; he rang the bell of a great double door, and Martins was aware of many voices beyond it. He turned sharply to the driver and said, 'Where the hell . . . ?' but the driver was already half-way down the stairs, and already the door was opening. His eyes were dazzled from the darkness by the lights inside; he heard, but he could hardly see, the advance of Crabbin. 'Oh, Mr Dexter, we have been so anxious, but better late

66

than never. Let me introduce you to Miss Wilbraham and the Gräfin von Meyersdorf.'

A buffet laden with coffee cups; an urn steaming; a woman's face shiny with exertion; two young men with the happy intelligent faces of sixth-formers; and, huddled in the background, like faces in a family album, a multitude of the old-fashioned, the dingy, the earnest and cheery features of constant readers. Martins looked behind him, but the door had closed.

He said desperately to Mr Crabbin, 'I'm sorry, but –'

'Don't think any more about it,' Mr Crabbin said. 'One cup of coffee and then let's go on to the discussion. We have a very good gathering tonight. They'll put you on your mettle, Mr Dexter.' One of the young men placed a cup in his hand, the other shovelled in sugar before he could say he preferred his coffee unsweetened. The younger man breathed into his ear, 'Afterwards would you mind signing one of your books, Mr Dexter?' A large woman in black silk bore down upon him and said, 'I don't mind if the Gräfin does hear me, Mr Dexter, but I don't like your books, I don't approve of them. I think a novel should tell a good story.'

'So do I,' Martins said hopelessly.

'Now, Mrs Bannock, wait for question time.'

'I know I'm downright, but I'm sure Mr Dexter values *honest* criticism.'

An old lady, who he supposed was the Gräfin, said, 'I do not read many English books, Mr Dexter, but I am told that yours . . .'

'Do you mind drinking up?' Crabbin said and hustled him through into an inner room where a number of elderly people were sitting on a semi-circle of chairs with an air of sad patience.

Martins was not able to tell me very much about the meeting; his mind was still dazed with the death; when he looked up he expected to see at any moment the child Hansel and hear that persistent pedantic refrain, 'Papa, Papa.' Apparently Crabbin opened the proceedings, and, knowing Crabbin, I am sure that it was a very lucid, very fair and unbiased picture of the contemporary English novel. I have heard him give that talk so often, varied only by the emphasis given to the work of the particular English visitor. He would have touched lightly on various problems of technique – the point of view, the passage of time – and then he would have declared the meeting open for questions and discussion.

Martins missed the first question altogether, but luckily Crabbin filled the gap and answered it satisfactorily. A woman wearing a brown hat and a piece of fur round her throat said with passionate interest, 'May I ask Mr Dexter if he is engaged on a new work?'

'Oh, yes – yes.'

'May I ask the title?'

'"The Third Man",' Martins said and gained a spurious confidence as the result of taking that hurdle.

'Mr Dexter, could you tell us what author has chiefly influenced you?'

Martins, without thinking, said, 'Grey.' He meant of course the author of *Riders of the Purple Sage*, and he was pleased to find his reply gave general satisfaction – to all save an elderly Austrian who asked, 'Grey. What Grey? I do not know the name.'

Martins felt he was safe now and said, 'Zane Grey – I don't know any other,' and was mystified at the low subservient laughter from the English colony.

Crabbin interposed quickly for the sake of the Austrians, 'That is a little joke of Mr Dexter's. He meant the poet Gray – a gentle, mild, subtle genius – one can see the affinity.'

'And he is called Zane Grey?'

'That was Mr Dexter's joke. Zane Grey wrote what we call Westerns – cheap popular novelettes about bandits and cowboys.'

'He is not a great writer?'

'No, no. Far from it,' Mr Crabbin said. 'In the strict sense I would not call him a writer at all.' Martins told me that he felt the first stirrings of revolt at that statement. He had never regarded himself before as a writer, but Crabbin's self-confidence irritated him – even the way the light flashed back from Crabbin's spectacles seemed an added cause of vexation. Crabbin said, 'He was just a popular entertainer.'

'Why the hell not?' Martins said fiercely.

'Oh, well, I merely meant——'

'What was Shakespeare?'

Somebody with great daring said, 'A poet.'

'Have you ever read Zane Grey?'

'No, I can't say——'

'Then you don't know what you are talking about.'

One of the young men tried to come to Crabbin's rescue.

'And James Joyce, where would you put James Joyce, Mr Dexter?'

'What do you mean put? I don't want to put anybody anywhere,' Martins said. It had been a very full day: he had drunk too much with Colonel Cooler; he had fallen in love; a man had been murdered – and now he had the quite unjust feeling that he was being got at. Zane Grey was one of his heroes: he was damned if he was going to stand any nonsense.

'I mean would you put him among the really great?'

'If you want to know, I've never heard of him. What did he write?'

He didn't realize it, but he was making an enormous impression. Only a great writer could have taken so arrogant, so original a line. Several people wrote Zane Grey's name on the backs of envelopes and the Gräfin whispered hoarsely to Crabbin, 'How do you spell Zane?'

'To tell you the truth, I'm not quite sure.'

A number of names were simultaneously flung at Martins – little sharp pointed names like Stein, round pebbles like Woolf. A young Austrian with an intellectual black forelock called out, 'Daphne du Maurier,' and Mr Crabbin winced and looked sideways at Martins. He said in an undertone, 'Be gentle with them.'

A kind-faced woman in a hand-knitted jumper said wistfully, 'Don't you agree, Mr Dexter, that no one, no one has written about *feelings* so poetically as Virginia Woolf? In prose, I mean.'

Crabbin whispered, 'You might say something about the stream of consciousness.'

'Stream of what?'

A note of despair came into Crabbin's voice. 'Please, Mr Dexter, these people are your genuine admirers. They want to hear your views. If you knew how they have *besieged* the Institute.'

An elderly Austrian said, 'Is there any writer in England today of the stature of the late John Galsworthy?'

There was an outburst of angry twittering in which the names of Du Maurier, Priestley, and somebody called Layman were flung to and fro. Martins sat gloomily back and saw again the snow, the stretcher, the desperate face of Frau Koch. He thought: if I had never returned, if I had never asked questions, would that little man still be alive? How had he benefited Harry by supplying another victim – a victim to assuage the fear of whom? – Herr Kurtz, Colonel Cooler (he could not believe that), Dr Winkler? Not one of them seemed adequate to the drab gruesome crime in the basement; he could hear the child saying, 'I saw blood on the coke,' and somebody turned towards him a blank face without features, a grey plasticine egg, the third man.

Martins could not have said how he got through the rest of the discussion. Perhaps Crabbin took the brunt; perhaps he was helped by some of the audience who got into an animated discussion about the film version of a popular American novel. He remembered very little more before Crabbin was making a final speech in his honour. Then one of the young men led him to a table stacked with books and asked him to sign them. 'We have only allowed each member one book.'

'What have I got to do?'

'Just a signature. That's all they expect. This is my copy of *The Curved Prow*. I would be so grateful if you'd just write a little something . . .'

Martins took his pen and wrote: 'From B. Dexter, author of *The Lone Rider of Santa Fé*,' and the young man read the sentence and blotted it with a puzzled expression. As Martins sat down and started signing Benjamin Dexter's title pages, he could see in a mirror the young man showing the inscription to Crabbin. Crabbin smiled weakly and stroked his chin, up and down, up and down. 'B. Dexter, B. Dexter, B. Dexter,' Martins wrote rapidly – it was not, after all, a lie. One by one the books

71

were collected by their owners; little half-sentences of delight and compliment were dropped like curtsies – was this what it was to be a writer? Martins began to feel distinct irritation towards Benjamin Dexter. The complacent, tiring, pompous ass, he thought, signing the twenty-seventh copy of *The Curved Prow*. Every time he looked up and took another book he saw Crabbin's worried speculative gaze. The members of the Institute were beginning to go home with their spoils: the room was emptying. Suddenly in the mirror Martins saw a military policeman. He seemed to be having an argument with one of Crabbin's young henchmen. Martins thought he caught the sound of his own name. It was then he lost his nerve and with it any relic of common sense. There was only one book left to sign; he dashed off a last 'B. Dexter' and made for the door. The young man, Crabbin, and the policeman stood together at the entrance.

'And this gentleman?' the policeman asked.

'It's Mr Benjamin Dexter,' the young man said.

'Lavatory. Is there a lavatory?' Martins said.

'I understand a Mr Rollo Martins came here in one of your cars.'

'A mistake. An obvious mistake.'

'Second door on the left,' the young man said.

Martins grabbed his coat from the cloakroom as he went and made down the stairs. On the first-floor landing he heard someone mounting the stairs and, looking over, saw Paine, whom I had sent to identify him. He opened a door at random and shut it behind him. He could hear Paine going by. The room where he stood was in darkness; a curious moaning sound made him turn and face whatever room it was.

He could see nothing and the sound had stopped. He made a tiny movement and once more it started, like an impeded breath. He remained still and the sound died away. Outside somebody called, 'Mr Dexter, Mr Dexter.' Then a new sound started. It was like somebody whispering – a long continuous monologue in the darkness. Martins said, 'Is anybody there?' and the sound stopped again. He could stand no more of it. He took out his lighter. Footsteps went by and down the stairs. He scraped and scraped at the little wheel and no light came. Somebody shifted in the dark, and something rattled in mid-air like a chain. He asked once more with the anger of fear, 'Is anybody there?' and only the click-click of metal answered him.

Martins felt desperately for a light switch, first to his right hand and then to his left. He did not dare go farther because he could no longer locate his fellow occupant; the whisper, the moaning, the click had all stopped. Then he was afraid that he had lost the door and felt wildly for the knob. He was far less afraid of the police than he was of the darkness, and he had no idea of the noise he was making.

Paine heard it from the bottom of the stairs and came back. He switched on the landing light, and the glow under the door gave Martins his direction. He opened the door and, smiling weakly at Paine, turned back to take a second look at the room. The eyes of a parrot chained to a perch stared beadily back at him. Paine said respectfully, 'We were looking for you, sir. Colonel Calloway wants a word with you.'

'I lost my way,' Martins said.

'Yes, sir. We thought that was what had happened.'

I had kept a very careful record of Martins' movements from the moment I knew that he had not caught the plane home. He had been seen with Kurtz, and at the Josefstadt Theatre; I knew about his visit to Dr Winkler and to Colonel Cooler, his first return to the block where Harry had lived. For some reason my man lost him between Cooler's and Anna Schmidt's flats; he reported that Martins had wandered widely, and the impression we both got was that he had deliberately thrown off his shadower. I tried to pick him up at the hotel and just missed him.

Events had taken a disquieting turn, and it seemed to me that the time had come for another interview. He had a lot to explain.

I put a good wide desk between us and gave him a cigarette. I found him sullen but ready to talk, within strict limits. I asked him about Kurtz and he seemed to me to answer satisfactorily. I then asked him about Anna Schmidt and I gathered from his reply that he must have been with her after visiting Colonel Cooler; that filled in one of the missing points. I tried him with Dr Winkler, and he answered readily enough. 'You've been getting around,' I said, 'quite a bit. And have you found out anything about your friend?'

'Oh, yes,' he said. 'It was under your nose but you didn't see it.'

'What?'

'That he was murdered.' That took me by surprise: I had at one time played with the idea of suicide, but I had ruled even that out.

'Go on,' I said. He tried to eliminate from his story all

mention of Koch, talking about an informant who had seen the accident. This made his story rather confusing, and I couldn't grasp at first why he attached so much importance to the third man.

'He didn't turn up at the inquest, and the others lied to keep him out.'

'Nor did your man turn up – I don't see much importance in that. If it was a genuine accident, all the evidence needed was there. Why get the other chap in trouble? Perhaps his wife thought he was out of town; perhaps he was an official absent without leave – people sometimes take unauthorized trips to Vienna from places like Klagenfurt. The delights of the great city, for what they are worth.'

'There was more to it than that. The little chap who told me about it – they've murdered him. You see, they obviously didn't know what else he had seen.'

'Now we have it,' I said. 'You mean Koch.'

'Yes.'

'As far as we know, you were the last person to see him alive.' I questioned him then, as I've written, to find out if he had been followed to Koch's by somebody who was sharper than my man and had kept out of sight. I said, 'The Austrian police are anxious to pin this on you. Frau Koch told them how disturbed her husband was by your visit. Who else knew about it?'

'I told Cooler.' He said excitedly, 'Suppose immediately I left he telephoned the story to someone – to the third man. They had to stop Koch's mouth.'

'When you told Colonel Cooler about Koch, the man was already dead. That night he got out of bed, hearing someone, and went downstairs—'

'Well, that rules me out. I was in Sacher's.'

'But he went to bed very early. Your visit brought back the migraine. It was soon after nine when he got up. You returned to Sacher's at nine-thirty. Where were you before that?'

He said gloomily, 'Wandering round and trying to sort things out.'

'Any evidence of your movements?'

'No.'

I wanted to frighten him, so there was no point in telling him that he had been followed all the time. I knew that he hadn't cut Koch's throat, but I wasn't sure that he was quite so innocent as he made out. The man who owns the knife is not always the real murderer.

'Can I have another cigarette?'

'Yes.'

He said, 'How did you know that I went to Koch's? That was why you pulled me in here, wasn't it?'

'The Austrian police——'

'They hadn't identified me.'

'Immediately you left Colonel Cooler's, he telephoned to me.'

'Then that lets him out. If he had been concerned, he wouldn't have wanted me to tell you my story – to tell Koch's story, I mean.'

'He might assume that you were a sensible man and would come to me with your story as soon as you learned of Koch's death. By the way, how did you learn of it?'

He told me promptly and I believed him. It was then I began to believe him altogether. He said, 'I still can't believe Cooler's concerned. I'd stake anything on his honesty. He's one of those Americans with a real sense of duty.'

'Yes,' I said, 'he told me about that when he phoned.

76

He apologized for it. He said it was the worst of having been brought up to believe in citizenship. He said it made him feel a prig. To tell you the truth, Cooler irritates me. Of course, he doesn't know that I know about his tyre deals.'

'Is he in a racket, too, then?'

'Not a very serious one. I daresay he's salted away twenty-five thousand dollars. But I'm not a good citizen. Let the Americans look after their own people.'

'I'm damned.' He said thoughtfully, 'Is that the kind of thing Harry was up to?'

'No. It was not so harmless.'

He said, 'You know, this business – Koch's death – has shaken me. Perhaps Harry did get mixed up in something bad. Perhaps he was trying to clear out again, and that's why they murdered him.'

'Or perhaps,' I said, 'they wanted a bigger cut of the spoils. Thieves fall out.'

He took it this time without any anger at all. He said, 'We won't agree about motives, but I think you check your facts pretty well. I'm sorry about the other day.'

'That's all right.' There are times when one has to make a flash decision – this was one of them. I owed him something in return for the information he had given me. I said, 'I'll show you enough of the facts in Lime's case for you to understand. But don't fly off the handle. It's going to be a shock.'

It couldn't help being a shock. The war and the peace (if you can call it peace) let loose a great number of rackets, but none more vile than this one. The black marketeers in food did at least supply food, and the same applied to all the other racketeers who provided articles in short supply at extravagant prices. But the penicillin racket was a different affair altogether. Penicillin in Austria was supplied only to the military hospitals; no civilian doctor, not even a civilian hospital, could obtain it by legal means. As the racket started, it was relatively harmless. Penicillin would be stolen by military orderlies and sold to Austrian doctors for very high sums – a phial would fetch anything up to seventy pounds. You might say that this was a form of distribution – unfair distribution because it benefited only the rich patient, but the original distribution could hardly have a claim to greater fairness.

This racket went on quite happily for a while. Occasionally an orderly was caught and punished, but the danger simply raised the price of penicillin. Then the racket began to get organized: the big men saw big money in it, and while the original thief got less for his spoils, he received instead a certain security. If anything happened to him he would be looked after. Human nature too has curious twisted reasons that the heart certainly knows nothing of. It eased the conscience of many small men to feel that they were working for an employer: they were almost as respectable soon in their own eyes as wage-earners; they were one of a group, and if there was guilt, the leaders bore the guilt. A racket works like a totalitarian party.

This I have sometimes called stage two. Stage three was when the organizers decided that the profits were not large enough. Penicillin would not always be impossible to obtain legitimately; they wanted more money and quicker money while the going was good. They began to dilute the penicillin with coloured water, and, in the case of penicillin dust, with sand. I keep a small museum in one drawer in my desk, and I showed Martins examples. He wasn't enjoying the talk, but he hadn't yet grasped

78

the point. He said, 'I suppose that makes the stuff useless.'

I said, 'We wouldn't worry so much if that was all, but just consider. You can be immunized from the effects of penicillin. At the best you can say that the use of this stuff makes a penicillin treatment for the particular patient ineffective in the future. That isn't so funny, of course, if you are suffering from V.D. Then the use of sand on a wound that requires penicillin – well, it's not healthy. Men have lost their legs and arms that way – and their lives. But perhaps what horrified me most was visiting the children's hospital here. They had bought some of this penicillin for use against meningitis. A number of children simply died, and a number went off their heads. You can see them now in the mental ward.'

He sat on the other side of the desk, scowling into his hands. I said, 'It doesn't bear thinking about very closely, does it?'

'You haven't showed me any evidence yet that Harry——'

'We are coming to that now,' I said. 'Just sit still and listen.' I opened Lime's file and began to read. At the beginning the evidence was purely circumstantial, and Martins fidgeted. So much consisted of coincidence – reports from agents that Lime had been at a certain place at a certain time; the accumulation of opportunities; his acquaintance with certain people. He protested once, 'But the same evidence would apply against me – now.'

'Just wait,' I said. For some reason Harry Lime had grown careless: he may have realized that we suspected him and got rattled. He held a quite distinguished position in the Relief Organization, and a man like that is the more easily rattled. We put one of our agents as an orderly in the British Military Hospital: we knew by this time the name of our go-between, but we had never succeeded in getting the line right back to the source. Anyway, I am not going to bother the reader now, as I bothered Martins then, with all the stages – the long tussle to win the confidence of the go-between, a man called Harbin. At last we had the screws on Harbin, and we twisted them until he squealed. This kind of police work is very similar to secret service work: you look for a double agent whom you can really control, and Harbin was the man for us. But even he only led us as far as Kurtz.

'Kurtz!' Martins exclaimed. 'But why haven't you pulled him in?'

'Zero hour is almost here,' I said.

Kurtz was a great step forward, for Kurtz was in direct communication with Lime – he had a small outside job in connection with international relief. With Kurtz, Lime sometimes put things on paper – if he was pressed. I showed Martins the photostat of a note. 'Can you identify that?'

'It's Harry's hand.' He read it through. 'I don't see anything wrong.'

'No, but now read this note from Harbin to Kurtz – which we dictated. Look at the date. This is the result.'

He read them both through twice.

'You see what I mean?' If one watched a world come to an end, a plane dive from its course, I don't suppose one would chatter, and a world for Martins had certainly come to an end, a world of easy friendship, hero-worship, confidence that had begun twenty years before in a school corridor. Every memory – afternoons in the long grass, the illegitimate shoots on Brickworth Common, the dreams, the walks, every shared experience–was simultaneously tainted, like the soil of an atomized town. One could not walk there with safety for a long while. While he sat there, looking at his hands and saying nothing, I fetched a precious bottle of whisky out of a cupboard and poured out two large doubles. 'Go on,' I said, 'drink that,' and he obeyed me as though I were his doctor. I poured him out another.

He said slowly, 'Are you certain that he was the real boss?'

'It's as far back as we have got so far.'

'You see, he was always apt to jump before he looked.'

I didn't contradict him, though that wasn't the impression he had before given of Lime. He was searching round for some comfort.

'Suppose,' he said, 'someone had got a line on him, forced him into this racket, as you forced Harbin to double-cross . . .'

'It's possible.'

'And they murdered him in case he talked when he was arrested.'

'It's not impossible.'

'I'm glad they did,' he said. 'I wouldn't have liked to hear Harry squeal.' He made a curious little dusting movement with his hand on his knee as much as to say, 'That's that.' He said, 'I'll be getting back to England.'

'I'd rather you didn't just yet. The Austrian police would make an issue if you tried to leave Vienna at the moment. You see, Cooler's sense of duty made him call them up too.'

'I see,' he said hopelessly.

'When we've found the third man . . .' I said.

81

'I'd like to hear *him* squeal,' he said. 'The bastard. The bloody bastard.'

[11]

After he left me, Martins went straight off to drink himself silly. He chose the Oriental to do it in, the dreary smoky little night club that stands behind a sham Eastern façade. The same semi-nude photographs on the stairs, the same half-drunk Americans at the bar, the same bad wine and extraordinary gins – he might have been in any third-rate night haunt in any other shabby capital of a shabby Europe. At one point of the hopeless early hours the International Patrol took a look at the scene, and a Russian soldier made a bolt for the stairs at the sight of them, moving with bent averted head like a small harvest animal. The Americans never stirred and nobody interfered with them. Martins had drink after drink; he would probably have had a woman too, but the cabaret performers had all gone home, and there were practically no women left in the place, except for one beautiful shrewd-looking French journalist who made one remark to her companion and fell contemptuously asleep.

Martins moved on: at Maxim's a few couples were dancing rather gloomily, and at a place called Chez Victor the heating had failed and people sat in overcoats drinking cocktails. By this time the spots were swimming in front of Martins' eyes, and he was oppressed by a sense of loneliness. His mind reverted to the girl in Dublin, and the one in Amsterdam. That was one thing that didn't fool you – the straight drink, the simple physical act: one didn't expect fidelity from a woman.

His mind revolved in circles – from sentiment to lust and back again from belief to cynicism.

The trams had stopped, and he set out obstinately on foot to find Harry's girl. He wanted to make love to her – just like that: no nonsense, no sentiment. He was in the mood for violence, and the snowy road heaved like a lake and set his mind on a new course towards sorrow, eternal love, renunciation. In the corner of a sheltering wall he was sick in the snow.

It must have been about three in the morning when he climbed the stairs to Anna's room. He was nearly sober by that time and had only one idea in his head, that she must know about Harry too. He felt that somehow this knowledge would pay the mortmain that memory levies on human beings, and he would stand a chance with Harry's girl. If you are in love yourself, it never occurs to you that the girl doesn't know: you believe you have told it plainly in a tone of voice, the touch of a hand. When Anna opened the door to him, with astonishment at the sight of him tousled on the threshold, he never imagined that she was opening the door to a stranger.

He said, 'Anna, I've found out everything.'

'Come in,' she said, 'you don't want to wake the house.' She was in a dressing-gown; the divan had become a bed, the kind of tumbled bed that showed how sleepless the occupant had been.

'Now,' she said, while he stood there, fumbling for words, 'what is it? I thought you were going to keep away. Are the police after you?'

'No.'

'You didn't really kill that man, did you?'

'Of course not.'

'You're drunk, aren't you?'

'I am a bit,' he said sulkily. The meeting seemed to be going on the wrong lines. He said angrily, 'I'm sorry.'

'Why? I would like a drink myself.'

He said, 'I've been with the British police. They are satisfied I didn't do it. But I've learned everything from them. Harry was in a racket – a bad racket.' He said hopelessly, 'He was no good at all. We were both wrong.'

'You'd better tell me,' Anna said. She sat down on the bed and he told her, swaying slightly beside the table where her typescript part still lay open at the first page. I imagine he told it to her pretty confusedly, dwelling chiefly on what had stuck most in his mind, the children dead with meningitis, and the children in the mental ward. He stopped and they were silent. She said, 'Is that all?'

'Yes.'

'You were sober when they told you? They really proved it?'

'Yes.' He added drearily, 'So that, you see, was Harry.'

'I'm glad he's dead now,' she said. 'I wouldn't have wanted him to rot for years in prison.'

'But can you understand how Harry – your Harry, my Harry – could have got mixed up . . . ?' He said hopelessly, 'I feel as though he had never really existed, that we'd dreamed him. Was he laughing at fools like us all the time?'

'He may have been. What does it matter?' she said. 'Sit down. Don't worry.' He had pictured himself comforting *her* – not this other way about. She said, 'If he was alive now, he might be able to explain, but we've got to remember him as he was to us. There are always so many things that one doesn't know about a person, even a person one loves – good things, bad things. We have to leave plenty of room for them.'

'Those children——'

She said angrily, 'For God's sake stop making people in *your* image. Harry was real. He wasn't just your hero and my lover. He was Harry. He was in a racket. He did bad things. What about it? He was the man we knew.'

He said, 'Don't talk such bloody wisdom. Don't you see that I love you?'

She looked at him in astonishment. 'You?'

'Yes, me. I don't kill people with fake drugs. I'm not a hypocrite who persuades people that I'm the greatest – I'm just a bad writer who drinks too much and falls in love with girls . . .'

She said, 'But I don't even know what colour your eyes are. If you'd rung me up just now and asked me whether you were dark or fair or wore a moustache, I wouldn't have known.'

'Can't you get him out of your mind?'

'No.'

He said, 'As soon as they've cleared up this Koch murder, I'm leaving Vienna. I can't feel interested any longer in whether Kurtz killed Harry – or the third man. Whoever killed him it was a kind of justice. Maybe I'd kill him myself under these circumstances. But you still love him. You love a cheat, a murderer.'

'I loved a man,' she said. 'I told you – a man doesn't alter because you find out more about him. He's still the same man.'

'I hate the way you talk. I've got a splitting headache, and you talk and talk . . .'

'I didn't ask you to come.'

'You make me cross.'

Suddenly she laughed. She said, 'You are so comic. You come here at three in the morning – a stranger – and say you love me. Then you get angry and pick a quarrel. What do you expect me to do – or say?'

'I haven't seen you laugh before. Do it again. I like it.'

'There isn't enough for two laughs,' she said.

He took her by the shoulders and shook her gently. He said, 'I'd make comic faces all day long. I'd stand on my head and grin at you between my legs. I'd learn a lot of jokes from the books on after-dinner speaking.'

'Come away from the window. There are no curtains.'

'There's nobody to see.' But automatically checking his statement, he wasn't quite so sure: a long shadow that had moved, perhaps with the movement of clouds over the moon, was motionless again. He said, 'You still love Harry, don't you?'

'Yes.'

'Perhaps I do. I don't know.' He dropped his hands and said, 'I'll be pushing off.'

He walked rapidly away. He didn't bother to see whether he was being followed, to check up on the shadow. But, passing by the end of a street, he happened to turn, and there just around the corner, pressed against a wall to escape notice, was a thick stocky figure. Martins stopped and stared. There was something familiar about that figure. Perhaps, he thought, I have grown unconsciously used to him during these last twenty-four hours; perhaps he is one of those who have so assiduously checked my movements. Martins stood there, twenty yards away, staring at the silent motionless figure in the dark side street who stared back at him. A police spy, perhaps, or an agent of those other men, those men who had corrupted Harry first and then killed him – even possibly, the third man?

It was not the face that was familiar, for he could not make out so much as the angle of the jaw; nor a movement, for the body was so still that he began to believe that the whole thing was an illusion caused by shadow. He called sharply, 'Do you want anything?' and there was no reply. He called again with the irascibility of drink, 'Answer, can't you,' and an answer came, for a window curtain was drawn petulantly back by some sleeper he had awakened, and the light fell straight across the narrow street and lit up the features of Harry Lime.

[12]

'Do you believe in ghosts?' Martins said to me.

'Do you?'

'I do now.'

'I also believe that drunk men see things – sometimes rats, sometimes worse.'

He hadn't come to me at once with his story – only the danger to Anna Schmidt tossed him back into my office, like something the sea had washed up, tousled, unshaven, haunted by an experience he couldn't understand. He said, 'If it had been just the face, I wouldn't have worried. I'd been thinking about Harry, and I might easily have mistaken a stranger. The light was turned off again at once, you see. I only got one glimpse, and the man made off down the street – if he was a man. There was no turning for a long way, but I was so startled I gave him another thirty yards' start. He came to one of those advertisement kiosks and for a moment moved out of sight. I ran after him. It only took me ten seconds to reach the kiosk, and he must have heard me running, but the strange thing was he never appeared again. I reached the kiosk. There wasn't anybody there. The street was empty. He couldn't have reached a doorway without my seeing him. He simply vanished.'

'A natural thing for ghosts – or illusions.'

'But I can't believe I was as drunk as all that!'

'What did you do then?'

'I had to have another drink. My nerves were all in pieces.'

'Didn't that bring him back?'

'No, but it sent me back to Anna's.'

I think he would have been ashamed to come to me with his absurd story if it had not been for the attempt on Anna Schmidt. My theory, when he did tell me his story, was that there had been a watcher – though it was drink and hysteria that had pasted on the man's face the features of Harry Lime. The watcher had noted his visit to Anna, and the member of the ring – the penicillin ring – had been warned by telephone. Events that night moved fast. You remember that Kurtz lived in the Russian zone – in the Second Bezirk to be exact, in a wide, empty, desolate street that runs down to the Prater Platz. A man like that had probably obtained his influential contacts. It was ruin for a Russian to be observed on very friendly terms with an American or an Englishman, but the Austrian was a potential ally – and in any case one doesn't fear the influence of the ruined and defeated.

You must understand that at this period cooperation between the Western Allies and the Russians had practically, though not yet completely, broken down.

The original police agreement in Vienna between the

Allies confined the military police (who had to deal with crimes involving allied personnel) to their particular zones, unless permission was given to them to enter the zone of another Power. This agreement worked well enough between the three Western Powers. I only had to get on the phone to my opposite number in the American or French zones before I sent in my men to make an arrest or pursue an investigation. During the first six months of the occupation it had worked reasonably well with the Russians: perhaps forty-eight hours would pass before I received permission, and in practice there are few occasions when it is necessary to work quicker than that. Even at home it is not always possible to obtain a search warrant or permission from one's superiors to detain a suspect with any greater speed. Then the forty-eight hours turned into a week or a fortnight, and I remember my American colleague suddenly taking a look at his records and discovering that there were forty cases dating back more than three months where not even an acknowledgement of his requests had been received. Then the trouble started. We began to turn down, or not to answer, the Russian requests, and sometimes without permission they would send in police, and there were clashes. . . . At the date of this story the Western Powers had more or less ceased to put in applications or reply to the Russian ones. This meant that if I wanted to pick up Kurtz it would be as well to catch him outside the Russian zone, though of course it was always possible his activities might offend the Russians and his punishment be more sudden and severe than any we should inflict. Well, the Anna Schmidt case was one of the clashes: when Rollo Martins went drunkenly back at four o'clock in the morning to tell Anna that he had seen the ghost of Harry, he was told by a frightened porter who had not yet gone back to sleep that she had been taken away by the International Patrol.

What happened was this. Russia, you remember, was in the chair as far as the Innere Stadt was concerned, and when Russia was in the chair, you expected certain irregularities. On this occasion, half-way through the patrol, the Russian policeman pulled a fast one on his colleagues and directed the car to the street where Anna Schmidt lived. The British military policeman that night was new to his job: he didn't realize, till his colleagues told him, that they had entered a British zone. He spoke a little German and no French, and the Frenchman, a cynical hard-bitten Parisian, gave up the attempt to explain to him. The American took on the job. 'It's all right by me,' he said, 'but is it all right by you?' The British M.P. tapped the Russian's shoulder, who turned his Mongol face and launched a flood of incomprehensible Slav at him. The car drove on.

Outside Anna Schmidt's block the American took a hand in the game and demanded in German what it was all about. The Frenchman leaned against the bonnet and lit a stinking Caporal. France wasn't concerned, and anything that didn't concern France had no genuine importance to him. The Russian dug out a few words of German and flourished some papers. As far as they could tell, a Russian national wanted by the Russian police was living there without proper papers. They went upstairs and the Russian tried Anna's door. It was firmly bolted, but he put his shoulder to it and tore out the bolt without giving the occupant an opportunity of letting him in. Anna was in bed, though I don't suppose, after Martins' visit, she was asleep.

There is a lot of comedy in these situations if you are not directly concerned. You need a background of Central European terror, of a father who belonged to a losing side, of house-searches and disappearances, before the fear outweighs the comedy. The Russian, you see, refused to leave the room while Anna dressed: the Englishman refused to remain in the room: the American wouldn't leave a girl unprotected with a Russian soldier, and the Frenchman – well, I think the Frenchman must have thought it was fun. Can't you imagine the scene? The Russian was just doing his duty and watched the girl all the time, without a flicker of sexual interest; the American stood with his back chivalrously turned, but aware, I am sure, of every movement; the Frenchman smoked his cigarette and watched with detached amusement the reflection of the girl dressing in the mirror of the wardrobe; and the Englishman stood in the passage wondering what to do next.

I don't want you to think the English policeman came too badly out of the affair. In the passage, undistracted by chivalry, he had time to think, and his thoughts led him to the telephone in the next flat. He got straight through to me at my flat and woke me out of that deepest middle sleep. That was why when Martins rang up an hour later I already knew what was exciting him; it gave him an undeserved but very useful belief in my efficiency. I never heard another crack from him about policemen or sheriffs after that night.

I must explain another point of police procedure. If the International Patrol made an arrest, they had to lodge their prisoner for twenty-four hours at the International Headquarters. During that period it would be determined which Power could justifiably claim the prisoner.

It was this rule that the Russians were most ready to break. Because so few of us can speak Russian and the Russian is almost debarred from explaining his point of view (try and explain your own point of view on any subject in a language you don't know well – it's not as easy as ordering a meal), we are apt to regard any breach of an agreement by the Russians as deliberate and malign. I think it quite possible that they understood this agreement as referring only to prisoners about whom there was a dispute. It's true that there was a dispute about nearly every prisoner they took, but there was no dispute in their own minds, and no one has a greater sense of self-righteousness than a Russian. Even in his confessions a Russian is self-righteous – he pours out his revelations, but he doesn't excuse himself, he needs no excuse. All this had to form the background of one's decision. I gave my instructions to Corporal Starling.

When he went back to Anna's room a dispute was raging. Anna had told the American that she had Austrian papers (which was true) and that they were quite in order (which was rather stretching the truth). The American told the Russian in bad German that they had no right to arrest an Austrian citizen. He asked Anna for her papers and when she produced them, the Russian snatched them from her hand.

'Hungarian,' he said, pointing at Anna. 'Hungarian,' and then, flourishing the papers, 'bad, bad.'

The American, whose name was O'Brien, said, 'Give the goil back her papers,' which the Russian naturally didn't understand. The American put his hand on his gun, and Corporal Starling said gently, 'Let it go, Pat.'

'If these papers ain't in order we got a right to look.'

'Just let it go. We'll see the papers at H.Q.'

'If you get to H.Q. You can't trust these Russian drivers. As like as not he'll drive straight through to his zone.

'We'll see,' Starling said.

'The trouble about you British is you never know when to make a stand.'

'Oh, well,' Starling said; he had been at Dunkirk, but he knew when to be quiet.

They got back into the car with Anna, who sat in the front between the two Russians dumb with fear. After they had gone a little way the American touched the Russian on the shoulder, 'Wrong way,' he said. 'H.Q. that way.' The Russian chattered back in his own tongue making a conciliatory gesture, while they drove on. 'It's what I said,' O'Brien told Starling. 'They are taking her to the Russian zone.' Anna stared out with terror through the windscreen. 'Don't worry, little goil,' O'Brien said, 'I'll fix them all right.' His hand was fidgeting round his gun again. Starling said, 'Look here, Pat, this is a British case. You don't have to get involved.'

'You are new to this game. You don't know these bastards.'

'It's not worth making an incident about.'

'For Christ's sake,' O'Brien said, 'not worth . . .that little goil's got to have protection.' American chivalry is always, it seems to me, carefully canalized – one still awaits the American saint who will kiss a leper's sores.

The driver put on his brakes suddenly: there was a road block. You see, I knew they would have to pass this military post if they did not make their way to the International H.Q. in the Inner City. I put my head in at the window and said to the Russian haltingly, in his own

93

tongue, 'What are you doing in the British zone?'

He grumbled that it was 'orders'.

'Whose orders? Let me see them.' I noted the signature – it was useful information. I said, 'This tells you to pick up a certain Hungarian national and war criminal who is living with faulty papers in the British zone. Let me see the papers.'

He started on a long explanation, but I saw the papers sticking in his pocket and I pulled them out. He made a grab at his gun, and I punched his face – I felt really mean at doing so, but it's the conduct they expect from an angry officer and it brought him to reason – that and seeing three British soldiers approaching his headlights. I said, 'These papers look to me quite in order, but I'll investigate them and send a report of the result to your colonel. He can, of course, ask for the extradition of this lady at any time. All we want is proof of her criminal activities. I'm afraid we don't regard Hungarian as Russian nationality.' He goggled at me (my Russian was probably half incomprehensible) and I said to Anna, 'Get out of the car.' She couldn't get by the Russian, so I had to pull him out first. Then I put a packet of cigarettes in his hand, said, 'Have a good smoke,' waved my hand to the others, gave a sigh of relief, and that incident was closed.

[13]

While Martins told me how he went back to Anna's and found her gone, I did some hard thinking. I wasn't satisfied with the ghost story or the idea that the man with Harry Lime's features had been a drunken illusion. I took out two maps of Vienna and compared them. I rang up my assistant and, keeping Martins silent with a glass

94

of whisky, asked him if he had located Harbin yet. He said no; he understood he'd left Klagenfurt a week ago to visit his family in the adjoining zone. One always wants to do everything oneself; one has to guard against blaming one's juniors. I am convinced that I would never have let Harbin out of our clutches, but then I would probably have made all kinds of mistakes that my junior would have avoided. 'All right,' I said. 'Go on trying to get hold of him.'

'I'm sorry, sir.'

'Forget it. It's just one of those things.'

His young enthusiastic voice – if only one could still feel that enthusiasm for a routine job; how many opportunities, flashes of insight one misses simply because a job has become just a job – tingled up the wire. 'You know, sir, I can't help feeling that we ruled out the possibility of murder too easily. There are one or two points——'

'Put them on paper, Carter.'

'Yes, sir. I think, sir, if you don't mind my saying so,' (Carter is a very young man) 'we ought to have him dug up. There's no real evidence that he died just when the others said.'

'I agree, Carter. Get on to the authorities.'

Martins was right. I had made a complete fool of myself, but remember that police work in an occupied city is not like police work at home. Everything is unfamiliar: the methods of one's foreign colleagues, the rules of evidence, even the procedure at inquests. I suppose I had got into the state of mind when one trusts too much to one's personal judgement. I had been immensely relieved by Lime's death. I was satisfied with the accident.

I said to Martins, 'Did you look inside the kiosk or was it locked?'

'Oh, it wasn't a newspaper kiosk,' he said. 'It was one of those solid iron kiosks you see everywhere plastered with posters.'

'You'd better show me the place.'

'But is Anna all right?'

'The police are watching the flat. They won't try anything else yet.'

I didn't want to make a fuss in the neighbourhood with a police car, so we took trams – several trams – changing here and there, and came into the district on foot. I didn't wear my uniform, and I doubted anyway, after the failure of the attempt on Anna, whether they would risk a watcher. 'This is the turning,' Martins said and led me down a side street. We stopped at the kiosk. 'You see, he passed behind here and simply vanished – into the ground.'

'That was exactly where he did vanish to,' I said.

'How do you mean?'

An ordinary passer-by would never have noticed that the kiosk had a door, and of course it had been dark when the man disappeared. I pulled the door open and showed Martins the little curling iron staircase that disappeared into the ground. He said, 'Good God, then I didn't imagine him!'

'It's one of the entrances to the main sewer.'

'And anyone can go down?'

'Anyone. For some reason the Russians object to these being locked.'

'How far can one go?'

'Right across Vienna. People used them in air raids; some of our prisoners hid for two years down there. Deserters have used them – and burglars. If you know your way about you can emerge again almost anywhere in the city through a manhole or a kiosk like this one. The Austrians have to have special police for patrolling these sewers.' I closed the door of the kiosk again. I said, 'So that's how your friend Harry disappeared.'

'You really believe it was Harry?'

'The evidence points that way.'

'Then whom did they bury?'

'I don't know yet, but we soon shall, because we are digging him up again. I've got a shrewd idea, though, that Koch wasn't the only inconvenient man they murdered.'

Martins said, 'It's a bit of a shock.'

'Yes.'

'What are you going to do about it?'

'I don't know. It's no good applying to the Russians, and you can bet he's hiding out now in the Russian zone. We have no line now on Kurtz, for Harbin's blown – he must have been blown or they wouldn't have staged that mock death and funeral.'

'But it's odd, isn't it, that Koch didn't recognize the dead man's face from the window?'

'The window was a long way up and I expect the face had been damaged before they took the body out of the car.'

He said thoughtfully, 'I wish I could speak to him. You see, there's so much I simply can't believe.'

'Perhaps you are the only one who could speak to him. It's risky though, because you know too much.'

'I still can't believe – I only saw the face for a moment.' He said, 'What shall I do?'

'He won't leave the Russian zone now. Perhaps that's

why he tried to have the girl taken over – because he
loves her ? Because he doesn't feel secure ? I don't know.
I do know that the only person who could persuade him
to come over would be you – or her, if he still believes
you are his friend. But first you've got to speak to him. I
can't see the line.'

'I could go and see Kurtz. I have the address.'

I said, 'Remember. Lime may not want you to leave
the Russian zone when once you are there, and I can't
protect you there.'

'I want to clear the whole damned thing up,' Martins
said, 'but I'm not going to act as a decoy. I'll talk to him.
That's all.'

[14]

Sunday had laid its false peace over Vienna; the wind
had dropped and no snow had fallen for twenty-four
hours. All the morning trams had been full, going out to
Grinzing where the young wine is drunk and to the
slopes of snow on the hills outside. Walking over the
canal by the makeshift military bridge, Martins was
aware of the emptiness of the afternoon: the young were
out with their toboggans and their skis, and all around
him was the after-dinner sleep of age. A notice board
told him that he was entering the Russian zone, but there
were no signs of occupation. You saw more Russian
soldiers in the Inner City than here.

Deliberately he had given Kurtz no warning of his
visit. Better to find him out than a reception prepared for
him. He was careful to carry with him all his papers,
including the *laissez-passer* of the Four Powers that on
the face of it allowed him to move freely through all
the zones of Vienna. It was extraordinarily quiet over

here on the other side of the canal, and a melodramatic journalist had painted a picture of silent terror, but the truth was simply the wider streets, the greater shell damage, the fewer people – and Sunday afternoon. There was nothing to fear, but all the same, in this huge empty street where all the time you heard your own feet moving, it was difficult not to look behind.

He had no difficulty in finding Kurtz's block, and when he rang the bell the door was opened quickly, as though Kurtz expected a visitor, by Kurtz himself.

'Oh,' Kurtz said, 'it's you, Mr Martins,' and made a perplexed motion with his hand to the back of his head. Martins had been wondering why he looked so different, and now he knew. Kurtz was not wearing the toupée, and yet his head was not bald. He had a perfectly normal head of hair cut close. He said, 'It would have been better to have telephoned to me. You nearly missed me; I was going out.'

'May I come in a moment?'

'Of course.'

In the hall a cupboard door stood open, and Martins saw Kurtz's overcoat, his raincoat, a couple of soft hats, and, hanging sedately on a peg like a wrap, Kurtz's toupée. He said, 'I'm glad to see your hair has grown,' and saw, in the mirror on the cupboard door, the hatred flame and blush on Kurtz's face. When he turned Kurtz smiled at him like a conspirator and said vaguely, 'It keeps the head warm.'

'Whose head?' Martins asked, for it had suddenly occurred to him how useful that toupée might have been on the day of the accident. 'Never mind,' he went quickly on, for his errand was not with Kurtz. 'I'm here to see Harry.'

'Harry?'

'I want to talk to him.'

'Are you mad?'

'I'm in a hurry, so let's assume that I am. Just make a note of my madness. If you should see Harry – or his ghost – let him know that I want to talk to him. A ghost isn't afraid of a man, is it? Surely it's the other way round. I'll be waiting in the Prater by the Big Wheel for the next two hours – if you can get in touch with the dead, hurry.' He added, 'Remember, I was Harry's friend.'

Kurtz said nothing, but somewhere, in a room off the hall, somebody cleared his throat. Martins threw open a door; he had half expected to see the dead rise yet again, but it was only Dr Winkler who rose from a kitchen chair, in front of the kitchen stove, and bowed very stiffly and correctly with the same celluloid squeak.

'Dr Winkle,' Martins said. Dr Winkler looked extraordinarily out of place in a kitchen. The debris of a snack lunch littered the kitchen table, and the unwashed dishes consorted very ill with Dr Winkler's cleanness.

'Winkler,' the doctor corrected him with stony patience.

Martins said to Kurtz, 'Tell the doctor about my madness. He might be able to make a diagnosis. And remember the place – by the Great Wheel. Or do ghosts only rise by night?' He left the flat.

For an hour he waited, walking up and down to keep warm, inside the enclosure of the Great Wheel; the smashed Prater with its bones sticking crudely through the snow was nearly empty. One stall sold thin flat cakes like cartwheels, and the children queued with their coupons. A few courting couples would be packed together in a single car of the Wheel and revolve slowly above the city, surrounded by empty cars. As the car reached the highest point of the Wheel, the revolutions would stop for a couple of minutes and far overhead the tiny faces would press against the glass. Martins wondered who would come for him. Was there enough friendship left in Harry for him to come alone, or would a squad of police arrive? It was obvious from the raid on Anna Schmidt's flat that he had a certain pull. And then as his watch-hand passed the hour, he wondered: Was it all an invention of my mind? Are they digging up Harry's body now in the Central Cemetery?

Somewhere behind the cakestall a man was whistling, and Martins knew the tune. He turned and waited. Was it fear or excitement that made his heart beat – or just the memories that tune ushered in, for life had always quickened when Harry came, came just as he came now, as though nothing much had happened, nobody had been lowered into a grave or found with cut throat in a basement, came with his amused, deprecating, take-it-or-leave-it manner – and of course one always took it.

'Harry.'

'Hullo, Rollo.'

Don't picture Harry Lime as a smooth scoundrel. He wasn't that. The picture I have of him on my files is an excellent one: he is caught by a street photographer with his stocky legs apart, big shoulders a little hunched, a belly that has known too much good food for too long, on his face a look of cheerful rascality, a geniality, a recognition that *his* happiness will make the world's day. Now he didn't make the mistake of putting out a hand that might have been rejected, but instead just patted Martins on the elbow and said, 'How are things?'

'We've got to talk, Harry.'

'Of course.'

'Alone.'

'We couldn't be more alone than here.'

He had always known the ropes, and even in the smashed pleasure park he knew them, tipping the woman in charge of the Wheel, so that they might have a car to themselves. He said, 'Lovers used to do this in the old days, but they haven't the money to spare, poor devils, now,' and he looked out of the window of the swaying, rising car at the figures diminishing below with what looked like genuine commiseration.

Very slowly on one side of them the city sank; very slowly on the other the great cross-girders of the Wheel rose into sight. As the horizon slid away the Danube became visible, and the piers of the Reichsbrücke lifted above the houses. 'Well,' Harry said, 'it's good to see you, Rollo.'

'I was at your funeral.'

'That was pretty smart of me, wasn't it?'

'Not so smart for your girl. She was there too – in tears.'

'She's a good little thing,' Harry said. 'I'm very fond of her.'

'I didn't believe the police when they told me about you.'

Harry said, 'I wouldn't have asked you to come if I'd known what was going to happen, but I didn't think the police were on to me.'

'Were you going to cut me in on the spoils?'

'I've never kept you out of anything, old man, yet.' He stood with his back to the door as the car swung upwards, and smiled back at Rollo Martins, who could remember him in just such an attitude in a secluded corner of the school-quad, saying, 'I've learned a way to get out at night. It's absolutely safe. You are the only one I'm letting in on it.' For the first time Rollo Martins looked back through the years without admiration, as he thought: He's never grown up. Marlowe's devils wore squibs attached to their tails: evil was like Peter Pan – it carried with it the horrifying and horrible gift of eternal youth.

Martins said, 'Have you ever visited the children's hospital? Have you seen any of your victims?'

Harry took a look at the toy landscape below and came away from the door. 'I never feel quite safe in these things,' he said. He felt the back of the door with his hand, as though he were afraid that it might fly open and launch him into that iron-ribbed space. 'Victims?' he asked. 'Don't be melodramatic, Rollo. Look down there,' he went on, pointing through the window at the people moving like black flies at the base of the Wheel. 'Would you really feel any pity if one of those dots stopped moving – for ever? If I said you can have twenty thousand pounds for every dot that stops, would you really, old man, tell me to keep my money – without hesitation? Or would you calculate how many dots you could afford to spare? Free of income tax, old man. Free of income tax.' He gave his boyish conspiratorial smile. 'It's the only way to save nowadays.'

'Couldn't you have stuck to tyres?'

'Like Cooler? No, I've always been ambitious.'

'You are finished now. The police know everything.'

'But they can't catch me, Rollo, you'll see. I'll pop up again. You can't keep a good man down.'

The car swung to a standstill at the highest point of

the curve and Harry turned his back and gazed out of the window. Martins thought: One good shove and I could break the glass, and he pictured the body falling, falling, through the iron struts, a piece of carrion dropping among the flies. He said, 'You know the police are planning to dig up your body. What will they find?'

'Harbin,' Harry replied with simplicity. He turned away from the window and said, 'Look at the sky.'

The car had reached the top of the Wheel and hung there motionless, while the stain of the sunset ran in streaks over the wrinkled papery sky beyond the black girders.

'Why did the Russians try to take Anna Schmidt?'

'She had false papers, old man.'

'Who told them?'

'The price of living in this zone, Rollo, is service. I have to give them a little information now and then.'

'I thought perhaps you were just trying to get her here – because she was your girl? Because you wanted her?'

Harry smiled. 'I haven't all that influence.'

'What would have happened to her?'

'Nothing very serious. She'd have been sent back to Hungary. There's nothing against her really. A year in a labour camp perhaps. She'd be infinitely better off in her own country than being pushed around by the British police.'

'She hasn't told them anything about you.'

'She's a good little thing,' Harry repeated with satisfaction and pride.

'She loves you.'

'Well, I gave her a good time while it lasted.'

'And I love her.'

'That's fine, old man. Be kind to her. She's worth it. I'm glad.' He gave the impression of having arranged everything to everybody's satisfaction. 'And you can help to keep her mouth shut. Not that she knows anything that matters.'

'I'd like to knock you through the window.'

'But you won't, old man. Our quarrels never last long. You remember that fearful one in the Monaco, when we swore we were through. I'd trust you anywhere, Rollo. Kurtz tried to persuade me not to come, but I know you. Then he tried to persuade me to, well, arrange an accident. He told me it would be quite easy in this car.'

'Except that I'm the stronger man.'

'But I've got the gun. You don't think a bullet wound would show when you hit *that* ground?' Again the car began to move, sailing slowly down, until the flies were midgets, were recognizable human beings. 'What fools we are, Rollo, talking like this, as if I'd do that to you – or you to me.' He turned his back and leaned his face against the glass. One thrust. . . . 'How much do you earn a year with your Westerns, old man?'

'A thousand.'

'Taxed. I earn thirty thousand free. It's the fashion. In these days, old man, nobody thinks in terms of human beings. Governments don't, so why should we? They talk of the people and the proletariat, and I talk of the mugs. It's the same thing. They have their five-year plans and so have I.'

'You used to be a Catholic.'

'Oh, I still *believe*, old man. In God and mercy and all that. I'm not hurting anybody's soul by what I do. The dead are happier dead. They don't miss much here, poor devils,' he added with that odd touch of genuine pity, as the car reached the platform and the faces of the doomed-to-be-victims, the tired pleasure-hoping Sunday faces, peered in at them. 'I could cut you in, you know. It would be useful. I have no one left in the Inner City.'

'Except Cooler? And Winkler?'

'You really mustn't turn policeman, old man.' They passed out of the car and he put his hand again on Martins' elbow. 'That was a joke. I know you won't. Have you heard anything of old Bracer recently?'

'I had a card at Christmas.'

'Those were the days, old man. Those were the days. I've got to leave you here. We'll see each other some-time. If you are in a jam, you can always get me at Kurtz's.' He moved away and, turning, waved the hand he had had the tact not to offer: it was like the whole past moving off under a cloud. Martins suddenly called after him, 'Don't trust me, Harry,' but there was too great a distance now between them for the words to carry.

[15]

'Anna was at the theatre,' Martins told me, 'for the Sunday matinée. I had to see the whole dreary comedy through a second time. About a middle-aged composer and an infatuated girl and an understanding – a terribly understanding – wife. Anna acted very badly – she wasn't much of an actress at the best of times. I saw her afterwards in her dressing-room, but she was badly fussed. I think she thought I was going to make a serious pass at her all the time, and she didn't want a pass. I told her Harry was alive – I thought she'd be glad and that I would hate to see how glad she was, but she sat in front of her make-up mirror and let the tears streak the grease-paint and I wished afterwards that she had been glad. She looked awful and I loved her. Then I told her about my interview with Harry, but she wasn't really paying much attention because when I'd finished she said, "I wish he was dead."

'"He deserves to be," I said.

'"I mean he would be safe then – from everybody."'

I asked Martins, 'Did you show her the photographs I gave you – of the children?'

'Yes. I thought, it's got to be kill or cure this time. She's got to get Harry out of her system. I propped the pictures up among the pots of grease. She couldn't avoid seeing them. I said, "The police can't arrest Harry unless they get him into this zone, and we've got to help."

'She said, "I thought he was your friend." I said, "He *was* my friend." She said, "I'll never help you to get Harry. I don't want to see him again, I don't want to hear his voice. I don't want to be touched by him, but I won't do a thing to harm him."

'I felt bitter – I don't know why, because after all I had done nothing for her. Even Harry had done more for her than I had. I said, "You want him still," as though I were accusing her of a crime. She said, "I don't want him, but he's in me. That's a fact – not like friendship. Why, when I have a sex dream, he's always the man."'

I prodded Martins on when he hesitated. 'Yes?'

'Oh, I just got up and left her then. Now it's your turn to work on me. What do you want me to do?'

'I want to act quickly. You see, it was Harbin's body in the coffin, so we can pick up Winkler and Cooler right away. Kurtz is out of our reach for the time being, and so is the driver. We'll put in a formal request to the Russians for permission to arrest Kurtz and Lime: it makes our files tidy. If we are going to use you as our decoy, your message must go to Lime straight away – not after you've hung around in this zone for twenty-four hours. As I see it, you were brought here for a grilling almost as soon as you got back into the Inner City; you heard then from me about Harbin; you put two and two together and you go and warn Cooler. We'll let Cooler slip for the sake of the bigger game – we have no evidence that he was in on the penicillin racket. He'll escape into the Second Bezirk to Kurtz, and Lime will know you've played the game. Three hours later you send a message that the police are after you: you are in hiding and must see him.'

'He won't come.'

'I'm not so sure. We'll choose our hiding place carefully – where he'll think there's a minimum of risk. It's worth trying. It would appeal to his pride and sense of humour if he could scoop you out. And it would stop your mouth.'

Martins said, 'He never used to scoop me out – at school.' It was obvious that he had been reviewing the past with care and coming to conclusions.

'That wasn't such serious trouble and there was no danger of your squealing.'

He said, 'I told Harry not to trust me, but he didn't hear.'

'Do you agree?'

He had given me back the photographs of the children and they lay on my desk. I could see him take a long look at them. 'Yes,' he said, 'I agree.'

All the arrangements went according to plan. We delayed arresting Winkler, who had returned from the Second Bezirk, until after Cooler had been warned. Martins enjoyed his short interview with Cooler. Cooler greeted him without embarrassment and with considerable patronage. 'Why, Mr Martins, it's good to see you. Sit down. I'm glad everything went off all right between you and Colonel Calloway. A very straight chap, Calloway.'

'It didn't,' Martins said.

'You don't bear any ill-will, I'm sure, about my letting him know about you seeing Koch. The way I figured it was this – if you were innocent you'd clear yourself right away, and if you were guilty, well, the fact that I liked you oughtn't to stand in the way. A citizen has his duties.'

'Like giving false evidence at an inquest.'

Cooler said, 'Oh, that old story. I'm afraid you are riled at me, Mr Martins. Look at it this way – you as a citizen, owing allegiance——'

'The police have dug up the body. They'll be after you and Winkler. I want you to warn Harry . . .'

'I don't understand.'

'Oh, yes, you do.' And it was obvious that he did. Martins left him abruptly. He wanted no more of that kindly humanitarian face.

It only remained then to bait the trap. After studying the map of the sewer system I came to the conclusion that a café anywhere near the main entrance of the great sewer, which was placed like all the others in an advertisement kiosk, would be the most likely spot to tempt Lime.

He had only to rise once again through the ground, walk fifty yards, bring Martins back with him, and sink again into the obscurity of the sewers. He had no idea that this method of evasion was known to us: he probably knew that one patrol of the sewer police ended before midnight, and the next did not start till two, and so at midnight Martins sat in the little cold café in sight of the kiosk, drinking coffee after coffee. I had lent him a revolver; I had men posted as close to the kiosk as I could, and the sewer police were ready when zero hour struck to close the manholes and start sweeping the sewers inwards from the edge of the city. But I intended, if I could, to catch him before he went underground again. It would save trouble – and risk to Martins. So there, as I say, in the café Martins sat.

The wind had risen again, but it had brought no snow; it came icily off the Danube and in the little grassy square by the café it whipped up the snow like the surf on top of a wave. There was no heating in the café, and Martins sat warming each hand in turn on a cup of ersatz coffee – innumerable cups. There was usually one of my men in the café with him, but I changed them every twenty minutes or so irregularly. More than an hour passed. Martins had long given up hope and so had I, where I waited at the end of a phone several streets away, with a party of the sewer police ready to go down if it became necessary. We were luckier than Martins because we were warm in our great boots up to the thighs and our reefer jackets. One man had a small searchlight about half as big again as a car headlight strapped to his breast, and another man carried a brace of Roman candles. The telephone rang. It was Martins. He said, 'I'm perishing with cold. It's a quarter past one. Is there any point in going on with this?'

'You shouldn't telephone. You must stay in sight.'

'I've drunk seven cups of this filthy coffee. My stomach won't stand much more.'

'He can't delay much longer if he's coming. He won't want to run into the two o'clock patrol. Stick it another quarter of an hour, but keep away from the telephone.'

Martins' voice said suddenly, 'Christ, he's here! He's——' and then the telephone went dead. I said to my assistant, 'Give the signal to guard all manholes,' and to my sewer police, 'We are going down.'

What had happened was this. Martins was still on the telephone to me when Harry Lime came into the café. I don't know what he heard, if he heard anything. The mere sight of a man wanted by the police and without friends in Vienna speaking on the telephone would have been enough to warn him. He was out of the café again before Martins had put down the receiver. It was one of those rare moments when none of my men was in the café. One had just left and another was on the pavement about to come in. Harry Lime brushed by him and made for the kiosk. Martins came out of the café and saw my man. If he had called out then it would have been an easy shot, but I suppose it was not Lime, the penicillin racketeer, who was escaping down the street; it was Harry. Martins hesitated just long enough for Lime to put the kiosk between them; then he called out 'That's him,' but Lime had already gone to ground.

What a strange world unknown to most of us lies under our feet: we live above a cavernous land of waterfalls and rushing rivers, where tides ebb and flow as in the world above. If you have ever read the adventures of Allan Quatermain and the account of his voyage along the underground river to the city of Milosis, you will be able to picture the scene of Lime's last stand. The main sewer, half as wide as the Thames, rushes by under a huge arch, fed by tributary streams: these streams have fallen in waterfalls from higher levels and have been purified in their fall, so that only in these side channels is the air foul. The main stream smells sweet and fresh with a faint tang of ozone, and everywhere in the darkness is the sound of falling and rushing water. It was just past high tide when Martins and the policeman reached the river: first the curving iron staircase, then a short passage so low they had to stoop, and then the shallow edge of the water lapped at their feet. My man shone his torch along the edge of the current and said, 'He's gone that way,' for just as a deep stream when it shallows at the rim leaves an accumulation of debris, so the sewer left in the quiet water against the wall a scum of orange peel, old cigarette cartons, and the like, and in this scum Lime had left his trail as unmistakably as if he had walked in mud. My policeman shone his torch ahead with his left hand, and carried his gun in his right. He said to Martins, 'Keep behind me, sir, the bastard may shoot.'

'Then why the hell should you be in front?'

'It's my job, sir.' The water came half-way up their legs as they walked; the policeman kept his torch pointing down and ahead at the disturbed trail at the sewer's edge. He said, 'The silly thing is the bastard doesn't stand a chance. The manholes are all guarded and we've cordoned off the way into the Russian zone. All our chaps have to do now is to sweep inwards down the side passages from the manholes.' He took a whistle out of his pocket and blew, and very far away, here and again there, came the notes of a reply. He said, 'They are all down here now. The sewer police, I mean. They know this place just as I know the Tottenham Court Road. I wish my old woman could see me now,' he said, lifting his torch for a moment to shine it ahead, and at that moment the shot came. The torch flew out of his hand and fell into the stream. He said, 'God blast the bastard!'

'Are you hurt?'

'Scraped my hand, that's all. A week off work. Here, take this other torch, sir, while I tie my hand up. Don't shine it. He's in one of the side passages.' For a long time the sound of the shot went on reverberating: when the last echo died a whistle blew ahead of them, and Martins' companion blew an answer.

Martins said, 'It's an odd thing – I don't even know your name.'

'Bates, sir.' He gave a low laugh in the darkness. 'This isn't my usual beat. Do you know the Horseshoe, sir?'

'Yes.'

'And the Duke of Grafton?'

'Yes.'

'Well, it takes a lot to make a world.'

Martins said, 'Let me come in front. I don't think he'll shoot at me, and I want to talk to him.'

'I had orders to look after you, sir. Careful.'

'That's all right.' He edged round Bates, plunging a foot deeper in the stream as he went. When he was in front he called out, 'Harry,' and the name sent up an echo, 'Harry, Harry, Harry!' that travelled down the stream and woke a whole chorus of whistles in the darkness. He called again, 'Harry. Come out. It's no use.'

A voice startlingly close made them hug the wall. 'Is that you, old man?' it called. 'What do you want me to do?'

'Come out. And put your hands above your head.'

'I haven't a torch, old man. I can't see a thing.'

'Be careful, sir,' Bates said.

'Get flat against the wall. He won't shoot at me,' Martins said. He called, 'Harry, I'm going to shine the torch. Play fair and come out. You haven't got a chance.' He flashed the torch on, and twenty feet away, at the edge of the light and the water, Harry stepped into view. 'Hands above the head, Harry.' Harry raised his hand and fired. The shot ricocheted against the wall a foot from Martins' head, and he heard Bates cry out. At the same moment a searchlight from fifty yards away lit the whole channel, caught Harry in its beams, then Martins, then the staring eyes of Bates slumped at the water's edge with the sewage washing to his waist. An empty cigarette carton wedged into his armpit and stayed. My party had reached the scene.

Martins stood dithering there above Bates's body, with Harry Lime half-way between us. We couldn't shoot for fear of hitting Martins, and the light of the searchlight dazzled Lime. We moved slowly on, our revolvers trained for a chance, and Lime turned this way and that like a rabbit dazzled by headlights; then suddenly he took a flying jump into the deep central rushing stream. When we turned the searchlight after him he was submerged, and the current of the sewer carried him rapidly on, past the body of Bates, out of the range of the searchlight into the dark. What makes a man, without hope, cling to a few more minutes of existence? Is it a good quality or a bad one? I have no idea.

Martins stood at the outer edge of the searchlight beam, staring downstream. He had his gun in his hand now, and he was the only one of us who could fire with safety. I thought I saw a movement and called out to him, 'There. There. Shoot.' He lifted his gun and fired, just as he had fired at the same command all those years ago on Brickworth Common, fired, as he did then, inaccurately. A cry of pain came tearing back like calico down the cavern: a reproach, an entreaty. 'Well done,' I called and halted by Bates's body. He was dead. His eyes remained blankly open as we turned the searchlight on him; somebody stooped and dislodged the carton and threw it in the river, which whirled it on – a scrap of yellow Gold Flake: he was certainly a long way from the Tottenham Court Road.

I looked up and Martins was out of sight in the darkness. I called his name and it was lost in a confusion of echoes, in the rush and the roar of the underground river. Then I heard a third shot.

Martins told me later, 'I walked downstream to find Harry, but I must have missed him in the dark. I was afraid to lift the torch: I didn't want to tempt him to shoot again. He must have been struck by my bullet just at the entrance of a side passage. Then I suppose he crawled up the passage to the foot of the iron stairs. Thirty feet above his head was the manhole, but he wouldn't have had the strength to lift it, and even if he had succeeded the police were waiting above. He must have known all that, but he was in great pain, and just as an animal creeps into the dark to die, so I suppose a man makes for the light. He wants to die at home, and the darkness is never home to *us*. He began to pull himself up the stairs, but then the pain took him and he couldn't go on. What made him whistle that absurd scrap of a tune I'd been fool enough to believe he had written himself? Was he trying to attract attention, did he want a friend with him, even the friend who had trapped him, or was he delirious and had he no purpose at all? Anyway I heard his whistle and came back along the edge of the stream, and felt where the wall ended and found my way up the passage where he lay. I said, "Harry," and the whistling stopped, just above my head. I put my hand on an iron hand-rail, and climbed. I was still afraid he might shoot. Then, only three steps up, my foot stamped down on his hand, and he was there. I shone my torch on him: he hadn't got a gun; he must have dropped it when my bullet hit him. For a moment I thought he was dead, but then he whimpered with pain. I said, "Harry," and he swivelled his eyes with a great effort to my face. He was trying to speak, and I bent down to listen. "Bloody fool," he said – that was all. I don't know whether he meant that for himself – some sort of act of contrition, however inadequate (he was a Catholic) – or was it for me – with my thousand a year taxed and my imaginary cattle-rustlers who couldn't even shoot a rabbit clean? Then he began to whimper again. I couldn't bear it any more and I put a bullet through him.'

'We'll forget that bit,' I said.

Martins said, 'I never shall.'

[17]

A thaw set in that night, and all over Vienna the snow melted, and the ugly ruins came to light again; steel rods hanging like stalactites, and rusty girders thrusting like bones through the grey slush. Burials were much simpler than they had been a week before when electric drills had been needed to break the frozen ground. It was almost as warm as a spring day when Harry Lime had his second funeral. I was glad to get him under earth again, but it had taken two men's deaths. The group by the grave was smaller now: Kurtz wasn't there, nor Winkler – only the girl and Rollo Martins and myself. And there weren't any tears.

After it was over the girl walked away without a word to either of us down the long avenue of trees that led to the main entrance and the tram stop, splashing through the melted snow. I said to Martins, 'I've got transport. Can I give you a lift?'

'No,' he said, 'I'll take a tram back.'

'You win. You've proved me a bloody fool.'

'I haven't won,' he said. 'I've lost.' I watched him striding off on his overgrown legs after the girl. He caught her up and they walked side by side. I don't think he said a word to her: it was like the end of a story except that before they turned out of my sight her hand was through his arm – which is how a story usually begins. He was a very bad shot and a very bad judge of character, but he had a way with Westerns (a trick of tension) and with girls (I wouldn't know what). And Crabbin? Oh, Crabbin is still arguing with the British Council about Dexter's expenses. They say they can't pass simultaneous payments in Stockholm and Vienna. Poor Crabbin. Poor all of us, when you come to think of it.

LOSER TAKES ALL

Dear Frere,
As we have been associated in business and friendship for a quarter of a century I am dedicating this frivolity without permission to you. Unlike some of my Catholic critics, you, I know, when reading this little story, will not mistake me for 'I', nor do I need to explain to you that this tale has not been written for the purposes of encouraging adultery, the use of pyjama tops, or registry office marriages. Nor is it meant to discourage gambling.

Affectionately and gratefully,

Graham Greene

PART ONE

[1]

I suppose the small greenish statue of a man in a wig on a horse is one of the famous statues of the world. I said to Cary, 'Do you see how shiny the right knee is? It's been touched so often for luck, like St Peter's foot in Rome.'

She rubbed the knee carefully and tenderly as though she were polishing it. 'Are you superstitious?' I said.

'Yes.'

'I'm not.'

'I'm so superstitious I never walk under ladders. I throw salt over my right shoulder. I try not to tread on the cracks in pavements. Darling, you're marrying the most superstitious woman in the world. Lots of people aren't happy. We are. I'm not going to risk a thing.'

'You've rubbed that knee so much, we ought to have plenty of luck at the tables.'

'I wasn't asking for luck at the tables,' she said.

[2]

That night I thought that our luck had begun in London two weeks before. We were to be married at St Luke's Church, Maida Hill, and we were going to Bournemouth for the honeymoon. Not, on the face of it, an exhilarating programme, but I thought I didn't care a damn where we went so long as Cary was there. Le Touquet was within our means, but we thought we could be more alone in

Bournemouth – the Ramages and the Truefitts were going to Le Touquet. 'Besides, you'd lose all our money at the Casino,' Cary said, 'and we'd have to come home.'

'I know too much about figures. I live with them all day.'

'You won't be bored at Bournemouth?'

'No. I won't be bored.'

'I wish it wasn't your second honeymoon. Was the first very exciting – in Paris?'

'We could only afford a week-end,' I said guardedly.

'Did you love her a terrible lot?'

'Listen,' I said, 'it was more than fifteen years ago. You hadn't started school. I couldn't have waited all that time for you.'

'But did you?'

'The night after she left me I took Ramage out to dinner and stood him the best champagne I could get. Then I went home and slept for nine hours right across the bed. She was one of those people who kick at night and then say you are taking up too much room.'

'Perhaps I'll kick.'

'That would feel quite different. I hope you'll kick. Then I'll know you are there. Do you realize the terrible amount of time we'll waste asleep, not knowing a thing? A quarter of our life.'

It took her a long time to calculate that. She wasn't good at figures as I was. 'More,' she said, 'much more. I like ten hours.'

'That's even worse,' I said. 'And eight hours at the office without you. And food – this awful business of having meals.'

'I'll try to kick,' she said.

That was at lunch-time the day when our so-called

luck started. We used to meet as often as we could for a snack at the Volunteer which was just round the corner from my office – Cary drank cider and had an unquenchable appetite for cold sausages. I've seen her eat five and then finish off with a hard-boiled egg.

'If we were rich,' I said, 'you wouldn't have to waste time cooking.'

'But think how much more time we'd waste eating. These sausages – look, I'm through already. We shouldn't even have finished the caviare.'

'And then the *sole meunière*,' I said.

'A little fried spring chicken with new peas.'

'A *soufflé Rothschild*.'

'Oh, don't be rich, please,' she said. 'We mightn't like each other if we were rich. Like me growing fat and my hair falling out . . .'

'That wouldn't make any difference.'

'Oh yes, it would,' she said. 'You know it would,' and the talk suddenly faded out. She was not too young to be wise, but she was too young to know that wisdom shouldn't be spoken aloud when you are happy.

I went back to the huge office block with its glass, glass, glass, and its dazzling marble floor and its pieces of modern carving in alcoves and niches like statues in a Catholic church. I was the assistant accountant (an ageing assistant accountant) and the very vastness of the place made promotion seem next to impossible. To be raised from the ground floor I would have to be a piece of sculpture myself.

In little uncomfortable offices in the city people die and people move on: old gentlemen look up from steel boxes and take a Dickensian interest in younger men. Here, in the great operational room with the computers ticking and the tape machines clicking and the soundless typewriters padding, you felt there was no chance for a man who hadn't passed staff college. I hadn't time to sit down before a loudspeaker said, 'Mr Bertram wanted in Room 10.' (That was me.)

'Who lives in Room 10?' I asked.

Nobody knew. Somebody said, 'It must be on the eighth floor.' (He spoke with awe as though he were referring to the peak of Everest – the eighth floor was as far as the London County Council regulations in those days allowed us to build towards Heaven.)

'Who lives in Room 10?' I asked the liftman again.

'Don't you know?' he said sourly: 'How long have you been here?'

'Five years.'

We began to mount. He said, 'You ought to know who lives in Room 10.'

'But I don't.'

'Five years and you don't know that.'

'Be a good chap and tell me.'

'Here you are. Eighth floor, turn left.' As I got out, he said gloomily, 'Not know Room 10!' He relented as he shut the gates. 'Who do you think? The Gom, of course.'

Then I began to walk very slowly indeed.

I have no belief in luck. I am not superstitious, but it is impossible, when you have reached forty and are conspicuously unsuccessful, not sometimes to half-believe in a malign providence. I had never met the Gom: I had only seen him twice; there was no reason so far as I could tell why I should ever see him again. He was elderly; he would die first, I would contribute grudgingly to a memorial. But to be summoned from the ground floor to the eighth shook me. I wondered what terrible mistake could justify a reprimand in Room 10; it seemed to be quite possible that our wedding now would never take place at St Luke's, nor our fortnight at Bournemouth. In a way I was right.

[3]

The Gom was called the Gom by those who disliked him and by all those too far removed from him for any feeling at all. He was like the weather – unpredictable. When a new tape machine was installed, or new computers replaced the old reliable familiar ones, you said, 'The Gom, I suppose,' before settling down to learn the latest toy. At Christmas little typewritten notes came round, addressed personally to each member of the staff (it must have given the typing pool a day's work, but the signature below the seasonal greeting, Herbert Dreuther, was rubber stamped). I was always a little surprised that the letter was not signed Gom. At that season of bonuses and cigars, unpredictable in amount, you sometimes heard him called by his full name, the Grand Old Man.

And there was something grand about him with his mane of white hair, his musician's head. Where other men collected pictures to escape death duties, he collected for pleasure. For a month at a time he would disappear in his yacht with a cargo of writers and actresses and oddments – a hypnotist, a man who had invented a new rose or discovered something about the endocrine glands. We on the ground floor, of course, would never have missed him: we should have known nothing about it if we had not read an account in the papers – the cheaper Sunday papers followed the progress of the yacht from port to port: they associated yachts with scandal, but there would never be any scandal on Dreuther's boat. He hated unpleasantness outside office hours.

I knew a little more than most from my position: diesel oil was included with wine under the general heading of Entertainment. At one time that caused trouble with Sir Walter Blixon. My chief told me about it. Blixon was the other power at No. 45. He held about as many shares as Dreuther, but he was not proportionally consulted. He was small, spotty, undistinguished, and consumed with jealousy. He could have had a yacht himself, but nobody would have sailed with him. When he objected to the diesel oil, Dreuther magnanimously gave way and then proceeded to knock all private petrol from the firm's account. As he lived in London he employed the firm's car, but Blixon had a house in Hampshire. What Dreuther courteously called a compromise was reached – things were to remain as they were. When Blixon managed somehow to procure himself a knighthood, he gained a momentary advantage until the rumour was said to have reached him that Dreuther had refused one in the same Honours List. One thing was certainly true – at a dinner party to which Blixon and my chief had been invited, Dreuther was heard to oppose a knighthood for a certain artist. 'Impossible. He couldn't accept it. An O.M. (or possibly a C.H.) are the only honours that remain respectable.' It made matters worse that Blixon had never heard of the C.H.

But Blixon bided his time. One more packet of shares would give him control and we used to believe that his chief prayer at night (he was a churchwarden in Hampshire) was that these shares would reach the market while Dreuther was at sea.

[4]

With despair in my heart I knocked on the door of No. 10 and entered, but even in my despair I memorized details – they would want to know them on the ground floor. The room was not like an office at all – there was a bookcase containing sets of English classics and it showed Dreuther's astuteness that Trollope was there and not Dickens, Stevenson and not Scott, thus giving an appearance of personal taste. There was an unimportant Renoir and a lovely little Boudin on the far wall, and one noticed at once that there was a sofa but not a desk. The few visible files were stacked on a Regency table, and Blixon and my chief and a stranger sat uncomfortably on the edge of easy chairs. Dreuther was almost out of sight – he lay practically on his spine in the largest and deepest chair, holding some papers above his head and scowling at them through the thickest glasses I have ever seen on a human face.

'It is fantastic and it cannot be true,' he was saying in his deep guttural voice.

'I don't see the importance . . .' Blixon said.

Dreuther took off his glasses and gazed across the room at me. 'Who are you?' he asked.

'This is Mr Bertram, my assistant,' the chief accountant said.

'What is he doing here?'

'You told me to send for him.'

'I remember,' Dreuther said. 'But that was half an hour ago.'

'I was out at lunch, sir.'

'Lunch?' Dreuther asked as though it were a new word.

'It was during the lunch hour, Mr Dreuther,' the chief accountant said.

'And they go out for lunch?'

'Yes, Mr Dreuther.'

'All of them?'

'Most of them, I think.'

'How very interesting. I did not know. Do you go out to lunch, Sir Walter?'

'Of course I do, Dreuther. Now, for goodness sake, can't we leave this in the hands of Mr Arnold and Mr Bertram? The whole discrepancy only amounts to seven pounds fifteen and fourpence. I'm hungry, Dreuther.'

'It's not the amount that matters, Sir Walter. You and I are in charge of a great business. We cannot leave our responsibilities to others. The shareholders . . .'

'You are talking highfalutin rubbish, Dreuther. The shareholders are you and I . . .'

'And the Other, Sir Walter. Surely you never forget the Other. Mr Bertrand, please sit down and look at these accounts. Did they pass through your hands?'

With relief I saw that they belonged to a small subsidiary company with which I did not deal. 'I have nothing to do with General Enterprises, sir.'

'Never mind. You may know something about figures – it is obvious that no one else does. Please see if you notice anything wrong.'

The worst was obviously over. Dreuther had exposed an error and he did not really worry about a solution. 'Have a cigar, Sir Walter. You see, you cannot do without me yet.' He lit his own cigar. 'You have found the error, Mr Bertrand?'

'Yes. In the General Purposes account.'

'Exactly. Take your time, Mr Bertrand.'

'If you don't mind, Dreuther, I have a table at the Berkeley . . .'

'Of course, Sir Walter, if you are so hungry . . . I can deal with this matter.'

'Coming, Naismith?' The stranger rose, made a kind of bob at Dreuther and sidled after Blixon.

'And you, Arnold, you have had no lunch?'

'It really doesn't matter, Mr Dreuther.'

'You must pardon me. It had never crossed my mind . . . this – lunch hour – you call it?'

'Really it doesn't . . .'

'Mr Bertrand has had lunch. He and I will worry out this problem between us. Will you tell Miss Bullen that I am ready for my glass of milk? Would you like a glass of milk, Mr Bertrand?'

'No thank you, sir.'

I found myself alone with the Gom. I felt exposed as he watched me fumble with the papers – on the eighth floor, on a mountain top, like one of those Old Testament characters to whom a King commanded, 'Prophesy.'

'Where do you lunch, Mr Bertrand?'

'At the Volunteer.'

'Is that a good restaurant?'

'It's a public house, sir.'

'They serve meals?'

'Snacks.'

'How very interesting.' He fell silent and I began all over again to add, carry, subtract. I was for a time puzzled. Human beings are capable of the most simple errors, the failing to carry a figure on, but we had all the best machines and a machine should be incapable . . .

'I feel at sea, Mr Bertrand,' Dreuther said.

'I confess, sir, I *am* a little too.'

'Oh, I didn't mean in that way, not in that way at all. There is no hurry. We will put all that right. In our good time. I mean that when Sir Walter leaves my room I have a sense of calm, peace. I think of my yacht.' The cigar smoke blew between us. '*Luxe, calme et volupté,*' he said.

'I can't find any *ordre* or *beauté* in these figures, sir.'

'You read Baudelaire, Mr Bertrand?'

'Yes.'

'He is my favourite poet.'

'I prefer Racine, sir. But I expect that is the mathematician in me.'

'Don't depend too much on his classicism. There are moments in Racine, Mr Bertrand, when – the abyss opens.' I was aware of being watched while I started checking all over again. Then came the verdict. 'How very interesting.'

But now at last I was really absorbed. I have never been able to understand the layman's indifference to figures. The veriest fool vaguely appreciates the poetry of the solar system – 'the army of unalterable law' – and yet he cannot see glamour in the stately march of the columns, certain figures moving upwards, crossing over, one digit running the whole length of every column, emerging, like some elaborate drill at Trooping the Colour. I was following one small figure now, dodging in pursuit.

'What computers do General Enterprises use, sir?'

'You must ask Miss Bullen.'

'I'm certain it's the Revolg. We gave them up five years ago. In old age they have a tendency to slip, but only when the 2 and the 7 are in relationship, and then not always, and then only in subtraction not addition. Now, here, sir, if you'll look, the combination happens four times, but only once has the slip occurred . . .'

'Please don't explain to me, Mr Bertrand. It would be useless.'

'There's nothing wrong except mechanically. Put these figures through one of our new machines. And scrap the Revolg (they've served long enough).'

I sat back on the sofa with a gasp of triumph. I felt the equal of any man. It had really been a very neat piece of detection. So simple when you knew, but everyone before me had accepted the perfection of the machine and no machine is perfect; in every join, rivet, screw lies original sin. I tried to explain that to Dreuther, but I was out of breath.

'How very interesting, Mr Bertrand. I'm glad we have solved the problem while Sir Walter is satisfying his carnal desires. Are you sure you won't have a glass of milk?'

'No thank you, sir. I must be getting back to the ground floor.'

'No hurry. You look tired, Mr Bertrand. When did you last have a holiday?'

'My annual leave's just coming round, sir. As a matter of fact I'm taking the opportunity to get married.'

'Really. How interesting. Have you received your clock?'

'Clock?'

'I believe they always give a clock here. The first time, Mr Bertrand?'

'Well . . . the second.'

'Ah, the second stands much more chance.'

The Gom had certainly a way with him. He made you talk, confide, he gave an effect of being really interested – and I think he always was, for a moment. He was a prisoner in his room, and small facts of the outer world came to him with the shock of novelty; he entertained them as an imprisoned man entertains a mouse or treasures a leaf blown through the bars. I said, 'We are going to Bournemouth for our honeymoon.'

'Ah, that I do not think is a good idea. That is *too* classical. You should take the young woman to the south – the bay of Rio de Janeiro . . .'

'I'm afraid I couldn't afford it, sir.'

'The sun would do you good, Mr Bertrand. You are pale. Some would suggest South Africa, but that is no better than Bournemouth.'

'I'm afraid that anyway . . .'

'I have it, Mr Bertrand. You and your beautiful young wife will come on my yacht. All my guests leave me at Nice and Monte Carlo. I will pick you up then on the 30th. We will sail down the coast of Italy, the Bay of Naples, Capri, Ischia.'

'I'm afraid, sir, it's a bit difficult. I'm very, very grateful, but you see we are getting married on the 30th.'

'Where?'

'St Luke's, Maida Hill.'

'St Luke's! You are being too classical again, my friend. We must not be too classical with a beautiful young wife. I assume she is young, Mr Bertrand?'

'Yes.'

'And beautiful?'

'I think so, sir.'

'Then you must be married at Monte Carlo. Before the mayor. With myself as witness. On the 30th. At night we sail for Portofino. That is better than St Luke's or Bournemouth.'

'But surely, sir, there would be legal difficulties . . .'

But he had already rung for Miss Bullen. I think he

would have made a great actor; he already saw himself in the part of a Haroun who could raise a man from obscurity and make him the ruler over provinces. I have an idea too that he thought it would make Blixon jealous. It was the same attitude which he had taken to the knighthood. Blixon was probably planning to procure the Prime Minister to dinner. This would show how little Dreuther valued rank. It would take the salt out of any social success Blixon might have.

Miss Bullen appeared with a second glass of milk. 'Miss Bullen, please arrange with our Nice office to have Mr Bertrand married in Monte Carlo on the 30th at 4 p.m.'

'On the 30th, sir?'

'There may be residence qualifications – they must settle those. They can include him on their staff for the last six months. They will have to see the British Consul too. You had better speak on the telephone to M. Tissand, but don't bother me about it. I want to hear no more of it. Oh, and tell Sir Walter Blixon that we have found an error in the Revolg machines. They have got to be changed at once. He had better consult Mr Bertrand who will advise him. I want to hear no more of that either. The muddle has given us a most exhausting morning. Well, Mr Bertrand, until the 30th then. Bring a set of Racine with you. Leave the rest to Miss Bullen. Everything is settled.' So he believed, of course, but there was still Cary.

[5]

The next day was a Saturday. I met Cary at the Volunteer and walked all the way home with her: it was one

135

of those spring afternoons when you can smell the country in a London street, tree smells and flower smells blew up into Oxford Street from Hyde Park, the Green Park, St James's, Kensington Gardens.

'Oh,' she said, 'I wish we could go a long, long way to somewhere very hot and very gay and very——' I had to pull her back or she would have been under a bus. I was always saving her from buses and taxis – sometimes I wondered how she kept alive when I wasn't there.

'Well,' I said, 'we can,' and while we waited for the traffic lights to change I told her.

I don't know why I expected such serious opposition: perhaps it was partly because she had been so set on a church wedding, the choir and the cake and all the nonsense. 'Think,' I said, 'to be married in Monte Carlo instead of Maida Hill. The sea down below and the yacht waiting . . .' As I had never been there, the details rather petered out.

She said, 'There's sea at Bournemouth too. Or so I've heard.'

'The Italian coast.'

'In company with your Mr Dreuther.'

'We won't share a cabin with him,' I said, 'and I don't suppose the hotel in Bournemouth will be quite empty.'

'Darling, I did want to be married at St Luke's.'

'Think of the Town Hall at Monte Carlo – the mayor in all his robes – the, the . . .'

'Does it count?'

'Of course it counts.'

'It would be rather fun if it didn't count, and then we could marry at St Luke's when we came back.'

'That would be living in sin.'

'I'd love to live in sin.'

136

'You could,' I said, 'any time. This afternoon.'

'Oh, I don't count London,' she said. 'That would be just making love. Living in sin is – oh, striped umbrellas and 80 in the shade and grapes – and a fearfully gay bathing suit. I'll have to have a new bathing suit.'

I thought all was well then, but she caught sight of one of those pointed spires sticking up over the plane trees a square ahead. 'We've sent out all the invitations. What will Aunt Marion say?' (She had lived with Aunt Marion ever since her parents were killed in the blitz.)

'Just tell her the truth. She'd much rather get picture-postcards from Italy than from Bournemouth.'

'It will hurt the Vicar's feelings.'

'Only to the extent of a fiver.'

'Nobody will really believe we are married.' She added a moment later (she was nothing if not honest), 'That will be fun.'

Then the pendulum swung again and she went thoughtfully on, 'You are only hiring your clothes. But my dress is being made.'

'There's time to turn it into an evening dress. After all, that's what it would have become anyway.'

The church loomed in sight: it was a hideous church, but no more hideous than St Luke's. It was grey and flinty and soot-stained, with reddish steps to the street the colour of clay and a text on a board that said, 'Come to Me all ye who are heavy laden,' as much as to say, 'Abandon Hope.' A wedding had just taken place, and there was a dingy high-tide line of girls with perambulators and squealing children and dogs and grim middle-aged matrons who looked as though they had come to curse.

I said, 'Let's watch. This might be happening to us.'

137

A lot of girls in long mauve dresses with lacy Dutch caps came out and lined the steps: they looked with fear at the nursemaids and the matrons and one or two giggled nervously – you could hardly blame them. Two photographers set up cameras to cover the entrance, an arch which seemed to be decorated with stone clover leaves, and then the victims emerged followed by a rabble of relatives.

'It's terrible,' Cary said, 'terrible. To think that might be you and me.'

'Well, you haven't an incipient goitre and I'm – well, damn it, I don't blush and I know where to put my hands.'

A car was waiting decorated with white ribbons and all the bridesmaids produced bags of paper rose petals and flung them at the young couple.

'They are lucky,' I said. 'Rice is still short, but I'm certain Aunt Marion can pull strings with the grocer.'

'She'd never do such a thing.'

'You can trust no one at a wedding. It brings out a strange atavistic cruelty. Now that they are not allowed to bed the bride, they try to damage the bridegroom. Look,' I said, clutching Cary's arm. A small boy, encouraged by one of the sombre matrons, had stolen up to the door of the car and, just as the bridegroom stooped to climb in, he launched at close range a handful of rice full in the unfortunate young man's face.

'When you can only spare a cupful,' I said, 'you are told to wait until you can see the white of your enemy's eyes.'

'But it's terrible,' Cary said.

'That, my dear child, is what is called a church marriage.'

138

'But ours wouldn't be like that. It's going to be very quiet – only near relatives.'

'You forget the highways and the hedges. It's a Christian tradition. That boy wasn't a relation. Trust me. I know. I've been married in church myself.'

'You were married in church? You never told me,' she said. 'In that case I'd *much* rather be married in a town hall. You haven't been married in a town hall too, have you?'

'No, it will be the first time – and the last time.'

'Oh, for God's sake,' Cary said, 'touch wood.'

So there she was two weeks later rubbing away at the horse's knee, asking for luck, and the great lounge of the Monte Carlo hotel spread emptily around us, and I said, 'That's that. We're alone, Cary.' (One didn't count the receptionist and the cashier and the concierge and the two men with our luggage and the old couple sitting on a sofa, for Mr Dreuther, they told me, had not yet arrived and we had the night to ourselves.)

[6]

We had dinner on the terrace of the hotel and watched people going into the Casino. Cary said, 'We ought to look in for the fun. After all, we aren't gamblers.'

'We couldn't be,' I said, 'not with fifty pounds basic.' We had decided not to use her allowance in case we found ourselves able to go to Le Touquet for a week in the winter.

'You are an accountant,' Cary said. 'You ought to know all the systems.'

'Systems are damned expensive,' I said. I had discovered that we had a suite already booked for us by Miss Bullen and I had no idea what it would cost. Our passports were still under different names, so I suppose it was reasonable that we should have two rooms, but the sitting-room seemed unnecessary. Perhaps we were supposed to entertain in it after the wedding. I said, 'You need a million francs* to play a system, and then you are up against the limit. The bank can't lose.'

'I thought someone broke the bank once.'

'Only in a comic song,' I said.

'It would be awful if we were really gamblers,' she said. 'You've got to care so much about money. You don't, do you?'

'No,' I said and meant it. All I had in my mind that night was the wonder whether we would sleep together. We never had. It was that kind of marriage. I had tried the other kind, and now I would have waited months if I could gain in that way all the rest of the years. But tonight I didn't want to wait any longer. I was as fussed as a young man – I found I could no longer see into Cary's mind. She was twenty years younger, she had never been married before, and the game was all in her hands. I couldn't even interpret what she said to me. For instance as we crossed to the Casino she said, 'We'll only stay ten minutes. I'm terribly tired.' Was that hint in my favour or against me? Or was it just a plain statement of fact? Had the problem in my mind never occurred to her, or had she already made up her mind so certainly that the problem didn't exist? Was she assuming I knew the reason?

I had thought when they showed us our rooms I would

* At the period of this story the franc stood at about 1200 francs to the pound.

discover, but all she had said with enormous glee was, 'Darling. What extravagance.'

I took the credit for Miss Bullen. 'It's only for one night. Then we'll be on the boat.' There was one huge double room and one very small single room and a medium-sized sitting-room in between: all three had balconies. I felt as though we had taken the whole front of the hotel. First she depressed me by saying, 'We could have two single rooms,' and then she contradicted that by saying, 'All the beds are double ones,' and then down I went again when she looked at the sofa in the sitting-room and said, 'I wouldn't have minded sleeping on that.' I was no wiser, and so we talked about systems. I didn't care a damn for systems.

After we had shown our passports and got our tickets we entered what they call the *cuisine*, where the small stakes are laid. 'This is where I belong,' Cary said, and nothing was less true. The old veterans sat around the tables with their charts and their pads and their pencils, making notes of every number. They looked, some of them, like opium smokers, dehydrated. There was a very tiny brown old lady with a straw hat of forty years ago covered in daisies: her left claw rested on the edge of the table like the handle of an umbrella and her right held a chip worth one hundred francs. After the ball had rolled four times she played her piece and lost it. Then she began waiting again. A young man leant over her shoulder, staked 100 on the last twelve numbers, won and departed. 'There goes a wise man,' I said, but when we came opposite the bar, he was there with a glass of beer and a sandwich. 'Celebrating three hundred francs,' I said.

'Don't be mean. Watch him, I believe that's the first food he's had today.'

I was on edge with wanting her, and I flared suddenly up; foolishly, for she would never have looked twice at him otherwise. So it is we prepare our own dooms. I said, 'You wouldn't call me mean if he weren't young and good-looking.'

'Darling,' she said with astonishment, 'I was only——' and then her mouth hardened. 'You *are* mean now,' she said. 'I'm damned if I'll apologize.' She stood and stared at the young man until he raised his absurd romantic hungry face and looked back at her. 'Yes,' she said, 'he is young, he is good-looking,' and walked straight out of the Casino. I followed saying, 'Damn, damn, damn,' under my breath. I knew now how we'd spend the night.

We went up in the lift in a dead silence and marched down the corridor and into the sitting-room.

'You can have the large room,' she said.

'No, you can.'

'The small one's quite big enough for me. I don't like huge rooms.'

'Then I'll have to change the luggage. They've put yours in the large room.'

'Oh, all right,' she said and went into it and shut the door without saying good night. I began to get angry with her as well as myself – 'a fine first night of marriage,' I said aloud, kicking my suitcase, and then I remembered we weren't married yet, and everything seemed silly and wasteful.

I put on my dressing-gown and went out on to my balcony. The front of the Casino was floodlit: it looked a cross between a Balkan palace and a super-cinema with the absurd statuary sitting on the edge of the green roof looking down at the big portico and the commissionaires;

everything stuck out in the white light as though projected in 3 D. In the harbour the yachts were all lit up, and a rocket burst in the air over the hill of Monaco. It was so stupidly romantic I could have wept.

'Fireworks, darling,' a voice said, and there was Cary on her balcony with all the stretch of the sitting-room between us. 'Fireworks,' she said, 'isn't that just our luck?' so I knew all was right again.

'Cary,' I said – we had to raise our voices to carry. 'I'm so sorry . . .'

'Do you think there'll be a Catherine-wheel?'

'I wouldn't be surprised.'

'Do you see the lights in the harbour?'

'Yes.'

'Do you think Mr Dreuther's arrived?'

'I expect he'll sail in at the last moment tomorrow.'

'Could we get married without him? I mean he's a witness, isn't he, and his engine might have broken down or he might have been wrecked at sea or there might be a storm or something.'

'I think we could manage without him.'

'You do think it's arranged all right, don't you?'

'Oh yes, Miss Bullen's done it all. Four o'clock tomorrow.'

'I'm getting hoarse, are you, from shouting? Come on to the next balcony, darling.'

I went into the sitting-room and out on to the balcony there. She said, 'I suppose we'll all have to have lunch together – you and me and your Gom?'

'If he gets in for lunch.'

'It would be rather fun, wouldn't it, if he were a bit late. I like this hotel.'

143

'We'd have just enough money for two days, I suppose.'

'We could always run up terrible bills,' she said, and then added, 'not so much fun really as living in sin, I suppose. I wonder if that young man's in debt.'

'I wish you'd forget him.'

'Oh, I'm not a bit interested in him, darling. I don't like young men. I expect I've got a father fixation.'

'Damn it, Cary,' I said, 'I'm not as old as that.

'Oh yes, you are,' she said, 'puberty begins at fourteen.'

'Then in fifteen years from tonight you may be a grandmother.'

'Tonight?' she said nervously, and then fell silent. The fireworks exploded in the sky. I said, 'There's your Catherine-wheel.'

She turned and looked palely at it.

'What are you thinking, Cary?'

'It's so strange,' she said. 'We are going to be together now for years and years and years. Darling, do you think we'll have enough to talk about?'

'We needn't only talk.'

'Darling, I'm serious. Have we got *anything* in common? I'm terribly bad at mathematics. And I don't understand poetry. You do.'

'You don't need to – you are the poetry.'

'No, but really – I'm serious.'

'We haven't dried up yet, and we've been doing nothing else but talk.'

'It would be so terrible,' she said, 'if we became a couple. You know what I mean. You with your paper. Me with my knitting.'

'You don't know how to knit.'

'Well, playing patience then. Or listening to the radio. Or watching television. We'll never have a television, will we?'

'Never.'

The rockets were dying down: there was a long pause: I looked away from the lights in the harbour. She was squatted on the floor of the balcony, her head against the side, and she was fast asleep. When I leant over I could touch her hair. She woke at once.

'Oh, how silly. I was dozing.'

'It's bed-time.'

'Oh. I'm not a bit tired really.'

'You said you were.'

'It's the fresh air. It's so nice in the fresh air.'

'Then come on my balcony.'

'Yes, I could, couldn't I?' she said dubiously.

'We don't need both balconies.'

'No.'

'Come round.'

'I'll climb over.'

'No. Don't. You might . . .'

'Don't argue,' she said, 'I'm here.'

They must have thought us crazy when they came to do the rooms – three beds for two people and not one of them had been slept in.

[7]

After breakfast we took a taxi to the Mairie – I wanted to be quite certain Miss Bullen had not slipped up, but everything was fixed; the marriage was to be at four sharp. They asked us not to be late as there was another wedding at 4.30.

'Like to go to the Casino?' I asked Cary. 'We could spend, say, 1,000 francs now that everything's arranged.'

'Let's take a look at the port first and see if he's come.' We walked down the steps which reminded me of Montmartre except that everything was so creamy and clean and glittering and new, instead of grey and old and historic. Everywhere you were reminded of the Casino – the bookshops sold systems in envelopes, '2,500 francs a week guaranteed', the toyshops sold small roulette boards, the tobacconists sold ashtrays in the form of a wheel, and even in the women's shops there were scarves patterned with figures and *manqué* and *pair* and *impair* and *rouge* and *noir*.

There were a dozen yachts in the harbour, and three carried British flags, but none of them was Dreuther's *Seagull*. 'Wouldn't it be terrible if he'd forgotten?' Cary said.

'Miss Bullen would never let him forget. I expect he's unloading passengers at Nice. Anyway last night you wanted him to be late.'

'Yes, but this morning it feels scary. Perhaps we oughtn't to play in the Casino – just in case.'

'We'll compromise,' I said. 'Three hundred francs. We can't leave Monaco without playing once.'

We hung around the *cuisine* for quite a while before we played. This was the serious time of day – there were no tourists and the *Salle Privée* was closed and only the veterans sat there. You had a feeling with all of them that their lunch depended on victory. It was a long, hard, dull employment for them – a cup of coffee and then to work till lunch-time – if their system was successful and

146

they could afford the lunch. Once Cary laughed – I forget what at, and an old man and an old woman raised their heads from opposite sides of the table and stonily stared. They were offended by our frivolity: this was no game to them. Even if the system worked, what a toil went into earning the 2,500 francs a week. With their pads and their charts they left nothing to chance, and yet over and over again chance nipped in and shovelled away their tokens.

'Darling, let's bet.' She put all her three hundred francs on the number of her age, and crossed her fingers for luck. I was more cautious: I put one *carré* on the same figure, and backed *noir* and *impair* with my other two. We both lost on her age, but I won on my others.

'Have you won a fortune, darling? How terribly clever.'

'I've won two hundred and lost one hundred.'

'Well, buy a cup of coffee. They always say you ought to leave when you win.'

'We haven't really won. We are down four bob.'

'*You've* won.'

Over the coffee I said, 'Do you know, I think I'll buy a system just for fun? I'd like to see just how they persuade themselves . . .'

'If anybody could think up a system, it should be you.'

'I can see the possibility if there were no limit to the stakes, but then you'd have to be a millionaire.'

'Darling, you won't really think one up, will you? It's fun pretending to be rich for two days, but it wouldn't be fun if it were true. Look at the guests in the hotel, they are rich. Those women with lifted faces and dyed hair and awful little dogs.' She said again with one of her flashes of disquieting wisdom, 'You seem to get afraid of being old when you're rich.'

'There may be worse fears when you are poor.'

'They are ones we are used to. Darling, let's go and look at the harbour again. It's nearly lunch-time. Perhaps Mr Dreuther's in sight. This place – I don't like it terribly.'

We leant over a belvedere and looked down at the harbour – there wasn't any change there. The sea was very blue and very still and we could hear the voice of a cox out with an eight – it came clearly over the water and up to us. Very far away, beyond the next headland, there was a white boat, smaller than a celluloid toy in a child's bath.

'Do you think that's Mr Dreuther?' Cary asked.

'It might be. I expect it is.'

But it wasn't. When we came back after lunch there was no *Seagull* in the harbour and the boat we had seen was no longer in sight: it was somewhere on the way to Italy. Of course there was no need for anxiety: even if he failed to turn up before night, we could still get married. I said, 'If he's been held up, he'd have telegraphed.'

'Perhaps he's simply forgotten,' Cary said.

'That's impossible,' I said, but my mind told me that nothing was impossible with the Gom.

I said, 'I think I'll tell the hotel we'll keep on one room – just in case.'

'The small room,' Cary said.

The receptionist was a little crass. '*One* room, sir?'

'Yes, one room. The small one.'

'The small one? For you and madame, sir?'

'Yes.' I had to explain. 'We are being married this afternoon.'

'Congratulations, sir.'

'Mr Dreuther was to have been here.'

'We've had no word from Mr Dreuther, sir. He usually lets us know . . .We were not expecting him.'

Nor was I now, but I did not tell Cary that. This, after all, Gom or no Gom, was our wedding day. I tried to make her return to the Casino and lose a few hundred, but she said she wanted to walk on the terrace and look at the sea. It was an excuse to keep a watch for the *Seagull*. And of course the *Seagull* never came. That interview had meant nothing, Dreuther's kindness had meant nothing, a whim had flown like a wild bird over the snowy waste of his mind, leaving no track at all. We were forgotten. I said, 'It's time to go to the Mairie.'

'We haven't even a witness,' Cary said.

'They'll find a couple,' I said with a confidence I did not feel.

I thought it would be gay to arrive in a horse-cab and we climbed romantically into a ramshackle vehicle outside the Casino and sat down under the off-white awning. But we'd chosen badly. The horse was all skin and bone and I had forgotten that the road was uphill. An old gentleman with an ear-appliance was being pushed down to the Casino by a middle-aged woman, and she made far better progress down than we made up. As they passed us I could hear her precise English voice. She must have been finishing a story. She said, 'and so they lived unhappily ever after'; the old man chuckled and said, 'Tell me that one again.' I looked at Cary and hoped she hadn't heard but she had. 'Darling,' I said, 'don't be superstitious, not today.'

'There's a lot of sense in superstition. How do you know fate doesn't send us messages – so that we can be prepared. Like a kind of code. I'm always inventing new ones. For instance' – she thought a moment – 'it will be lucky if a confectioner's comes before a flower shop. Watch your side.'

I did, and of course a flower shop came first. I hoped she hadn't noticed, but 'You can't cheat fate,' she said mournfully.

The cab went slower and slower: it would have been quicker to walk. I looked at my watch: we had only ten minutes to go. I said, 'You ought to have sacrificed a chicken this morning and found what omens there were in the entrails.'

'It's all very well to laugh,' she said. 'Perhaps our horoscopes don't match.'

'You wouldn't like to call the whole thing off, would you? Who knows? We'll be seeing a squinting man next.'

'Is that bad?'

'It's awful.' I said to the cabby, 'Please. A little faster. *Plus vite.*'

Cary clutched my arm. 'Oh,' she said.

'What's the matter?'

'Didn't you see him when he looked round. He's got a squint.'

'But, Cary, I was only joking.'

'That doesn't make any difference. Don't you see? It's what I said, you invent a code and fate uses it.'

I said angrily, 'Well, it doesn't make any difference. We are going to be too late anyway.'

'Too late?' She grabbed my wrist and looked at my watch. She said, 'Darling, we can't be late. Stop. *Arrêtez.* Pay him off.'

'We can't run uphill,' I said, but she was already out

of the cab and signalling wildly to every car that passed. No one took any notice. Fathers of families drove smugly by. Children pressed their noses on the glass and made faces at her. She said, 'It's no use. We've got to run.'

'Why bother? Our marriage was going to be unlucky – you've read the omens, haven't you?'

'I don't care,' she said, 'I'd rather be unlucky with you than lucky with anyone else.' That was the sudden way she had – of dissolving a quarrel, an evil mood, with one clear statement. I took her hand and we began to run. But we would never have made it in time if a furniture-van had not stopped and given us a lift all the way. Has anyone else arrived at their wedding sitting on an old-fashioned brass bedstead? I said, 'From now on brass bedsteads will always be lucky.'

She said, 'There's a brass bedstead in the small room at the hotel.'

We had two minutes to spare when the furniture man helped us out on to the little square at the top of the world. To the south there was nothing higher, I suppose, before the Atlas mountains. The tall houses stuck up like cacti towards the heavy blue sky, and a narrow terracotta street came abruptly to an end at the edge of the great rock of Monaco. A Virgin in pale blue with angels blowing round her like a scarf looked across from the church opposite, and it was warm and windy and very quiet and all the roads of our life had led us to this square.

I think for a moment we were both afraid to go in. Nothing inside could be as good as this, and nothing was. We sat on a wooden bench, and another couple soon sat down beside us, the girl in white, the man in black: I became painfully conscious that I wasn't dressed up. Then a man in a high stiff collar made a great deal of fuss about papers and for a while we thought the marriage wouldn't take place at all: then there was a to-do, because we had turned up without witnesses, before they consented to produce a couple of sad clerks. We were led into a large empty room with a chandelier, and a desk – a notice on the door said *Salle des Mariages*, and the mayor, a very old man who looked like Clemenceau, wearing a blue and red ribbon of office, stood impatiently by while the man in the collar read out our names and our birth-dates. Then the mayor repeated what sounded like a whole code of laws in rapid French and we had to agree to them – apparently they were the clauses from the *Code Napoléon*. After that the mayor made a little speech in very bad English about our duty to society and our responsibility to the State, and at last he shook hands with me and kissed Cary on the cheek, and we went out again past the waiting couple on to the little windy square.

It wasn't an impressive ceremony, there was no organ like at St Luke's and no wedding guests. 'I don't feel I've been married,' Cary said, but then she added, 'It's fun not feeling married.'

[8]

There are so many faces in streets and bars and buses and stores that remind one of Original Sin, so few that carry permanently the sign of Original Innocence. Cary's face was like that – she would always until old age look at the world with the eyes of a child. She was never bored: every day was a new day: even grief was eternal and every joy would last for ever. 'Terrible' was her favourite adjective – it wasn't in her mouth a *cliché* – there *was* terror in her pleasures, her fears, her anxieties, her laughter – the terror of surprise, of seeing something for the first time. Most of us only see resemblances, every situation has been met before, but Cary saw only differences, like a wine-taster who can detect the most elusive flavour.

We went back to the hotel and the *Seagull* hadn't come and Cary met this anxiety quite unprepared as though it were the first time we had felt it. Then we went to the bar and had a drink, and it might have been the first drink we had ever had together. She had an insatiable liking for gin and Dubonnet which I didn't share. I said, 'He won't be in now till tomorrow.'

'Darling, shall we have enough for the bill?'

'Oh, we can manage tonight.'

'We might win enough at the Casino.'

'We'll stick to the cheap room. We can't afford to risk much.'

I think we lost about two thousand francs that night and in the morning and in the afternoon we looked down at the harbour and the *Seagull* wasn't there. 'He *has* forgotten,' Cary said. 'He'd have telegraphed otherwise.' I knew she was right, and I didn't know what to do, and when the next day came I knew even less.

'Darling,' Cary said, 'we'd better go while we can still pay,' but I had secretly asked for the bill (on the excuse that we didn't want to play beyond our resources), and I knew that already we had insufficient. There was nothing to do but wait. I telegraphed to Miss Bullen and she replied that Mr Dreuther was at sea and out of touch. I was reading the telegram out to Cary as the old man with the ear-appliance sat on a chair at the top of the steps, watching the people go by in the late afternoon sun.

153

He asked suddenly, 'Do you know Dreuther?'

I said, 'Well, Mr Dreuther is my employer.'

'You think he is,' he said sharply. 'You are in Sitra, are you?'

'Yes.'

'Then I'm your employer, young man. Don't you put your faith in Dreuther.'

'You are Mr Bowles?'

'Of course I'm Mr Bowles. Go and find my nurse. It's time we went to the tables.'

When we were alone again, Cary asked, 'Who was that horrible old man? Is he really your employer?'

'In a way. In the firm we call him A.N.Other. He owns a few shares in Sitra – only a few, but they hold the balance between Dreuther and Blixon. As long as he supports Dreuther, Blixon can do nothing, but if Blixon ever managed to buy the shares, I'd be sorry for the Gom. A way of speaking,' I added. 'Nothing could make me sorry for him now.'

'He's only forgetful, darling.'

'Forgetfulness like that only comes when you don't care a damn about other people. None of us has a right to forget anyone. Except ourselves. The Gom never forgets himself. Oh hell, let's go to the Casino.'

'We can't afford to.'

'We are so in debt we may as well.'

That night we didn't bet much: we stood there and watched the veterans. The young man was back in the *cuisine*. I saw him change a thousand francs into tokens of a hundred, and presently when he'd lost those, he went out – no coffee or rolls for him that evening. Cary said, 'Do you think he'll go hungry to bed?'

'We all will,' I said, 'if the *Seagull* doesn't come.'

154

I watched them playing their systems, losing a little, gaining a little, and I thought it was strange how the belief persisted – that somehow you could beat the bank. They were like theologians, patiently trying to rationalize a mystery. I suppose in all lives a moment comes when we wonder – suppose after all there is a God, suppose the theologians are right. Pascal was a gambler, who staked his money on a divine system. I thought, I am a far better mathematician than any of these – is that why I don't believe in their mystery, and yet if this mystery exists, isn't it possible that I might solve it where they have failed? It was almost like a prayer when I thought: it's not for the sake of money – I don't want a fortune – just a few days with Cary free from anxiety.

Of all the systems round the table there was only one that really worked, and that did not depend on the so-called law of chance. A middle-aged woman with a big bird's nest of false blonde hair and two gold teeth lingered around the most crowded table. If anybody made a *coup* she went up to him and touching his elbow appealed quite brazenly – so long as the croupier was looking elsewhere – for one of his 200-franc chips. Perhaps charity, like a hunched back, is considered lucky. When she received a chip she would change it for two one-hundred-franc tokens, put one in her pocket and stake the other *en plein*. She couldn't lose her hundreds, and one day she stood to gain 3,500 francs. Most nights she must have left the table a thousand francs to the good from what she had in her pocket.

'Did you see her?' Cary asked as we walked to the bar for a cup of coffee – we had given up the gins and Dubonnets. 'Why shouldn't I do that too?'

'We haven't come to that.'

'I've made a decision,' Cary said. 'No more meals at the hotel.'

'Do we starve?'

'We have coffee and rolls at a café instead – or perhaps milk – it's more nourishing.'

I said sadly, 'It's not the honeymoon I'd intended. Bournemouth would have been better.'

'Don't fret, darling. Everything will be all right when the *Seagull* comes.'

'I don't believe in the *Seagull* any more.'

'Then what do we do when the fortnight's over?'

'Go to gaol, I should think. Perhaps the prison is run by the Casino and we shall have recreation hours round a roulette wheel.'

'Couldn't you borrow from the Other?'

'Bowles? He's never lent without security in his life. He's sharper than Dreuther and Blixon put together – otherwise they'd have had his shares years ago.'

'But there must be something we can do, darling?'

'Madam, there is.' I looked up from my cooling coffee and saw a small man in frayed and dapper clothes with co-respondent shoes. His nose seemed bigger than the rest of his face: the experience of a lifetime had swollen the veins and bleared the eyes. He carried jauntily under his arm a walking stick that had lost its ferrule, with a duck's head for a handle. He said with blurred courtesy, 'I think I am unpardonably intruding, but you have had ill-success at the tables and I carry with me good tidings, sir and madam.'

'Well,' Cary said, 'we were just going . . .' She told me later that his use of a biblical phrase gave her a touch of shivers, of *diablerie* – the devil at his old game of quoting scripture.

'It is better for you to stay, for I have shut in my mind here a perfect system. That system I am prepared to let you have for a mere ten thousand francs.'

'You are asking the earth,' I said. 'We haven't got that much.'

'But you are staying at the Hôtel de Paris. I have seen you.'

'It's a matter of currency,' Cary said quickly. 'You know how it is with the English.'

'One thousand francs.'

'No,' Cary said, 'I'm sorry.'

'I tell you what I'll do,' I said, 'I'll stand you a drink for it.'

'Whisky,' the little man replied sharply. I realized too late that whisky cost 500 francs. He sat down at the table with his stick between his knees so that the duck seemed to be sharing his drink. I said, 'Go on.'

'It is a very small whisky.'

'You won't get another.'

'It is very simple,' the little man said, 'like all great mathematical discoveries. You bet first on one number and when your number wins you stake your gains on the correct transversal of six numbers. The correct transversal on one is 31 to 36; on two 13 to 18; on three . . .'

'Why?'

'You can take it that I am right. I have studied very carefully here for many years. For five hundred francs I will sell you a list of all the winning numbers which came up last June.'

'But suppose the number doesn't come up?'

'You wait to start the system until it does.'

'It might take years.'

The little man got up, bowed and said, 'That is why

one must have capital. I had too little capital. If instead of five million I had possessed ten million I would not be selling you my system for a glass of whisky.'

He retired with dignity, the ferruleless stick padding on the polished floor, the duck staring back at us as though it wanted to stay.

'I think my system's better,' Cary said. 'If that woman can get away with it, I can . . .'

'It's begging. I don't like my wife to beg.'

'I'm only a new wife. And I don't count it begging – it's not money, only tokens.'

'You know there was something that man said which made me think. It's a pure matter of reducing what one loses and increasing what one gains.'

'Yes, darling. But in my system I don't lose anything.'

She was away for nearly half an hour and then she came back almost at a run. 'Darling, put away your doodles. I want to go home.'

'They aren't doodles. I'm working out an idea.'

'Darling, please come at once or I'm going to cry.'

When we were outside she dragged me up through the gardens, between the floodlit palm trees and the flower-beds like sugar sweets. She said, 'Darling, it was a terrible failure.'

'What happened?'

'I did exactly what that woman did. I waited till someone won a lot of money and then I sort of nudged his elbow and said, "Give." But he didn't give, he said quite sharply, "Go home to your mother," and the croupier looked up. So I went to another table. And the man there just said, "Later. Later. On the terrace." Darling, he thought I was a tart. And when I tried a third time – oh, it was terrible. One of those attendants who

158

light people's cigarettes touched me on my arm and said, "I think Mademoiselle has played enough for tonight." Calling me Mademoiselle made it worse. I wanted to fling my marriage lines in his face, but I'd left them in the bathroom at the hotel.'

'In the bathroom?'

'Yes, in my sponge bag, darling, because for some reason I never lose my sponge bag – I've had it for years and years. But that's not why I want to cry. Darling, please let's sit down on this seat. I can't cry walking about – it's like eating chocolate in the open air. You get so out of breath you can't taste the chocolate.'

'For goodness' sake,' I said. 'If that's not the worst let me know the worst. Do you realize we shall never be able to go into the Casino again – just when I've started on a system, a real system.'

'Oh, it's not as bad as that, darling. The attendant gave me such a nice wink at the door. I know *he* won't mind my going back – but I never want to go back, never.'

'I wish you'd tell me.'

'That nice young man saw it all.'

'What young man?'

'The hungry young man. And when I went out into the hall he followed me and said very sweetly, "Madame, I can only spare a token of one hundred francs, but it is yours."'

'You didn't take it?'

'Yes – I couldn't refuse it. He was so polite, and he was gone before I had time to thank him for it. And I changed it and used the francs in the slot machines at the entrance and I'm sorry I'm howling like this, but I simply can't help it, he was so terribly courteous, and he must be so terribly hungry and he's got a mind above money or he wouldn't have lent me a hundred francs, and when I'd won five hundred I looked for him to give him half and he'd gone.'

'You won five hundred? It'll pay for our coffee and rolls tomorrow.'

'Darling, you are so sordid. Don't you see that for ever after he'll think I was one of those old harpies like Bird's Nest in there?'

'I expect he was only making a pass.'

'You are so sexual. He was doing nothing of the kind. He's much too hungry to make a pass.'

'They say starvation sharpens the passions.'

[9]

We still had breakfast at the hotel in order to keep up appearances, but we found ourselves wilting even before the liftman. I have never liked uniforms – they remind me that there are those who command and those who are commanded – and now I was convinced that everybody in uniform knew that we couldn't pay the bill. We always kept our key with us, so that we might never have to go to the desk, and as we had changed all our travellers' cheques on our arrival, we didn't even have to approach the accountant. Cary had found a small bar called the Taxi Bar at the foot of one of the great staircases, and there we invariably ate our invariable lunch and our dinner. It was years before I wanted to eat rolls again and even now I always drink tea instead of coffee. Then, on our third lunch-time, coming out of the bar we ran into the assistant receptionist from the hotel who was passing along the street. He bowed and went by, but I knew that our hour had struck.

We sat in the gardens afterwards in the early evening sun and I worked hard on my system, for I felt as though I were working against time. I said to Cary, 'Give me a thousand francs. I've got to check up.'

'But, darling,' she said, 'do you realize we've only got five thousand left. Soon we shan't have anything even for rolls.'

'Thank God for that. I can't bear the sight of a roll.'

'Then let's change to ices instead. They don't cost any more. And, think, we can change our diet, darling. Coffee ices for lunch, strawberry ices for dinner. Darling, I'm longing for dinner.'

'If my system is finished in time, we'll have steaks . . .'

I took the thousand and went into the *cuisine*. Paper in hand I watched the table carefully for a quarter of an hour before betting and then quite quietly and steadily I lost, but when I had no more tokens to play my numbers came up in just the right order. I went out again to Cary. I said, 'The devil was right. It's a question of capital.'

She said sadly, 'You are getting like all the others.'

'What do you mean?'

'You think numbers, you dream numbers. You wake up in the night and say "*Zéro deux*". You write on bits of paper at meals.'

'Do you call them meals?'

'There are four thousand francs in my bag and they've got to last us till the *Seagull* comes. We aren't going to gamble any more. I don't believe in your system. A week ago you said you couldn't beat the bank.'

'I hadn't studied . . .'

'That's what the devil said – he'd studied. You'll be selling your system soon for a glass of whisky.'

She got up and walked back to the hotel and I didn't follow. I thought, a wife ought to believe in her husband to the bitter end and we hadn't been married a week; and then after a while I began to see her point of view. For the last few days I hadn't been much company, and what a life it had been – afraid to meet the porter's eye, and that was exactly what I met as I came into the hotel.

He blocked my way and said, 'The manager's compliments, sir, and could you spare him a few moments. In his room.' I thought: they can't send her to prison too, only me, and I thought: the Gom, that egotistical bastard on the eighth floor who has let us in for all this because he's too great to remember his promises. He makes the world and then he goes and rests on the seventh day and his creation can go to pot that day for all he cares. If only for one moment I could have had him in my power – if he could have depended on my remembering *him*, but it was as if I was doomed to be an idea of his, he would never be an idea of mine.

'Sit down, Mr Bertram,' the manager said. He pushed a cigarette box across to me. 'Smoke?' He had the politeness of a man who has executed many people in his time.

'Thanks,' I said.

'The weather has not been quite so warm as one would expect at this time of year.'

'Oh, better than England, you know.'

'I do hope you are enjoying your stay.' This, I supposed, was the routine – just to show there was no ill-feeling – one has one's duty. I wished he would come to an end.

'Very much, thank you.'

'And your wife too?'

'Oh yes. Yes.'

He paused, and I thought: now it comes. He said, 'By the way, Mr Bertram, I think this is your first visit?'

'Yes.'

'We rather pride ourselves here on our cooking. I don't think you will find better food in Europe.'

'I'm sure you're right.'

'I don't want to be intrusive, Mr Bertram, please forgive me if I am, but we have noticed that you don't seem to care for our restaurant, and we are very anxious that you and your wife should be happy here in Monte Carlo. Any complaint you might have – the service, the wine . . . ?'

'Oh, I've no complaint. No complaint at all.'

'I didn't think you would have, Mr Bertram. I have great confidence in our service here. I came to the conclusion – you will forgive me if I'm intrusive –'

'Yes. Oh yes.'

'I know that our English clients often have trouble over currency. A little bad luck at the tables can so easily upset their arrangements in these days.'

'Yes. I suppose so.'

'So it occurred to me, Mr Bertram, that perhaps – how shall I put it – you might be, as it were, a little – you will forgive me, won't you – well, short of funds?'

My mouth felt very dry now that the moment had come. I couldn't find the bold frank words I wanted to use. I said, 'Well,' and goggled across the desk. There was a portrait of the Prince of Monaco on the wall and a huge ornate inkstand on the desk and I could hear the train going by to Italy. It was like a last look at freedom.

The manager said, 'You realize that the Administration of the Casino and of this hotel are most anxious –

really most anxious – you realize we are in a very special position here, Mr Bertram, we are not perhaps' – he smiled at his fingernails – 'quite ordinary *hôteliers*. We have had clients here whom we have looked after for – well, thirty years' – he was incredibly slow at delivering his sentence. 'We like to think of them as friends rather than clients. You know here in the Principality we have a great tradition – well, of discretion, Mr Bertram. We don't publish names of our guests. We are the repository of many confidences.'

I couldn't bear the man's rigmarole any more. It had become less like an execution than like the Chinese water-torture. I said, 'We are quite broke – there's a confidence for you.'

He smiled again at his nails. 'That was what I suspected, Mr Bertram, and so I hope you will accept a small loan. For a friend of Mr Dreuther. Mr Dreuther is a very old client of ours and we should be most distressed if any friend of his failed to enjoy his stay with us.' He stood up, bowed and presented me with an envelope – I felt like a child receiving a good-conduct prize from a bishop. Then he led me to the door and said in a low confidential voice, 'Try our *Château Gruaud Larose* 1934: you will not be disappointed.'

I opened the envelope on the bed and counted the notes. I said, 'He's lent us 250,000 francs.'

'I don't believe it.'

'What it is to be a friend of the Gom. I wish I liked the bastard.'

'How will we ever repay it?'

'The Gom will have to help. He kept us here.'

'We'll spend as little as we can, won't we, darling?'

'But no more coffee and rolls. Tonight we'll have a

party – the wedding party.' I didn't care a damn about the *Gruaud Larose* 1934: I hired a car and we drove to a little village in the mountains called Peille. Everything was rocky grey and gorse-yellow in the late sun which flowed out between the cold shoulders of the hills where the shadows waited. Mules stood in the street and the car was too large to reach the inn, and in the inn there was only one long table to seat fifty people. We sat at it and watched the darkness come, and they gave us their own red wine which wasn't very good and fat pigeons roasted and fruit and cheese. The villagers laughed in the next room over their drinks, and soon we could hardly see the enormous hump of hills.

'Happy?'

'Yes.'

She said after a while, 'I wish we weren't going back to Monte Carlo. Couldn't we send the car home and stay? We wouldn't mind about toothbrushes tonight, and tomorrow we could go – shopping.' She said the last word with an upward inflexion as though we were at the Ritz and the Rue de la Paix round the corner.

'A toothbrush at Cartier's,' I said.

'Lanvin for two pyjama tops.'

'Soap at Guerlain.'

'A few cheap handkerchiefs in the Rue de Rivoli.' She said, 'I can't think of anything else we'd want, can you? Did you ever come to a place like this with Dirty?' Dirty was the name she always used for my first wife who had been dark and plump and sexy with pekingese eyes.

'Never.'

'I like being somewhere without footprints.'

I looked at my watch. It was nearly ten and there was

half an hour's drive back. I said, 'I suppose we'd better go.'

'It's not late.'

'Well, tonight I want to give my system a real chance. If I use 200-franc tokens I've got just enough capital.'

'You aren't going to the Casino?'

'Of course I am.'

'But that's stealing.'

'No it isn't. He gave us the money to enjoy ourselves with.'

'Then half of it's mine. You shan't gamble with my half.'

'Dear, be reasonable. I need the capital. The system needs the capital. When I've won you shall have the whole lot back with interest. We'll pay our bills, we'll come back here if you like for all the rest of our stay.'

'You'll never win. Look at the others.'

'They aren't mathematicians. I am.'

An old man with a beard guided us to our car through the dark arched streets: she wouldn't speak, she wouldn't even take my arm. I said, 'This is our celebration night, darling. Don't be mean.'

'What have I said that's mean?' How they defeat us with their silences: one can't repeat a silence or throw it back as one can a word. In the same silence we drove home. As we came out over Monaco the city was floodlit, the Museum, the Casino, the Cathedral, the Palace – the fireworks went up from the rock. It was the last day of a week of illuminations: I remembered the first day and our quarrel and the three balconies.

I said, 'We've never seen the *Salle Privée*. We must go there tonight.'

'What's special about tonight?' she said.

'*Le mari doit protection à sa femme, la femme obéissance à son mari.*'

'What on earth are you talking about?'

'You told the mayor you agreed to that. There's another article you agreed to – "The wife is obliged to live with her husband and to follow him wherever he judges it right to reside." Well, tonight we are damned well going to reside in the *Salle Privée.*'

'I didn't understand what he was saying.' The worst was always over when she consented to argue.

'Please, dear, come and see my system win.'

'I shall only see it lose,' she said and she spoke with strict accuracy.

At 10.30 exactly I began to play and to lose and I lost steadily. I couldn't change tables because this was the only table in the *Salle Privée* at which one could play with a 200-franc minimum. Cary wanted me to stop when I had lost half of the manager's loan, but I still believed that the moment would come, the tide turn, my figures prove correct.

'How much is left?' she asked.

'This.' I indicated the five two-hundred-franc tokens. She got up and left me: I think she was crying, but I couldn't follow her without losing my place at the table.

And when I came back to our rooms in the hotel I was crying too – there are occasions when a man can cry without shame. She was awake: I could tell by the way she had dressed herself for bed how coldly she was awaiting me. She never wore the bottoms of her pyjamas except to show anger or indifference, but when she saw me sitting there on the end of the bed, shaking with the effort to control my tears, her anger went. She said, 'Darling, don't take on so. We'll manage somehow.'

She scrambled out of bed and put her arms round me. 'Darling,' she said, 'I've been mean to you. It might happen to anybody. Look, we'll try the ices, not the coffee and rolls, and the *Seagull*'s sure to come. Sooner or later.'

'I don't mind now if it never comes,' I said.

'Don't be bitter, darling. It happens to everybody, losing.'

'But I haven't lost,' I said, 'I've won.'

She took her arms away. 'Won?'

'I've won five million francs.'

'Then why are you crying?'

'I'm laughing. We are rich.'

'Oh, you beast,' she said, 'and I was sorry for you,' and she scrambled back under the bedclothes.

PART TWO

[1]

One adapts oneself to money much more easily than to poverty: Rousseau might have written that man was born rich and is everywhere impoverished. It gave me great satisfaction to pay back the manager and leave my key at the desk. I frequently rang the bell for the pleasure of confronting a uniform without shame. I made Cary have an Elizabeth Arden treatment, and I ordered the *Gruaud Larose* 1934 (I even sent it back because it was not the right temperature). I had our things moved to a suite and I hired a car to take us to the beach. At the beach I hired one of the private bungalows where we could sunbathe, cut off by bushes and shrubs from the eyes of common people. There all day I worked in the sun (for I was not yet quite certain of my system) while Cary read (I had even bought her a new book).

I discovered that, as on the stock exchange, money bred money. I would now use ten-thousand-franc squares instead of two-hundred-franc tokens, and inevitably at the end of the day I found myself richer by several million. My good fortune became known: casual players would bet on the squares where I had laid my biggest stake, but they had not protected themselves, as I had with my other stakes, and it was seldom that they won. I noted a strange aspect of human nature, that though my system worked and theirs did not, the veterans never lost faith in their own calculations – not one abandoned his elaborate schemes, which led to nothing but loss, to follow my victorious method. The second day, when I had already increased my five million to nine, I heard an old lady say bitterly, 'What deplorable luck,' as though it were my good fortune alone that prevented the wheel revolving to her system.

On the third day I began to attend the Casino for longer hours – I would put in three hours in the morning in the kitchen and the same in the afternoon, and then of course in the evening I settled down to my serious labour in the *Salle Privée*. Cary had accompanied me on the second day and I had given her a few thousand francs to play with (she invariably lost them), but on the third day I thought it best to ask her to stay away. I found her anxious presence at my elbow distracting, and twice I made a miscalculation because she spoke to me. 'I love you very much, darling,' I said to her, 'but work is work. You go and sunbathe, and we'll see each other for meals.'

'Why do they call it a game of chance?' she said.

'How do you mean?'

'It's not a game. You said it yourself – it's work. You've begun to commute. Breakfast at nine thirty sharp, so as to catch the first table. What a lot of beautiful money you're earning. At what age will you retire?'

'Retire?'

'You mustn't be afraid of retirement, darling. We shall see so much more of each other, and we could fit up a little roulette wheel in your study. It will be so nice when you don't have to cross the road in all weathers.'

That night I brought my winnings up to fifteen million francs before dinner, and I felt it called for a celebration. I *had* been neglecting Cary a little – I realized that, so I thought we would have a good dinner and go to the ballet instead of my returning to the tables. I told her that and she seemed pleased. 'Tired businessman relaxes,' she said.

'As a matter of fact I am a little tired.' Those who have not played roulette seriously little know how fatiguing it can be. If I had worked less hard during the afternoon I wouldn't have lost my temper with the waiter in the bar. I had ordered two very dry Martinis and he brought them to us quite drowned in Vermouth – I could tell at once from the colour without tasting. To make matters worse he tried to explain away the colour by saying he had used Booth's gin. 'But you know perfectly well that I only take Gordon's,' I said, and sent them back. He brought me two more and he had put lemon peel in them. I said, 'For God's sake how long does one have to be a customer in this bar before you begin to learn one's taste?'

'I'm sorry, sir. I only came yesterday.'

I could see Cary's mouth tighten. I was in the wrong, of course, but I had spent a very long day at the Casino, and she might have realized that I am not the kind of man who is usually crotchety with servants. She said, 'Who would think that a week ago we didn't even dare to speak to a waiter in case he gave us a bill?'

When we went in to dinner there was a little trouble about our table on the terrace: we were earlier than usual, but as I said to Cary we had been good customers and they could have taken some small trouble to please. However, this time I was careful not to let my irritation show more than very slightly – I was determined that this dinner should be one to remember.

Cary as a rule likes to have her mind made up for her,

so I took the menu and began to order. 'Caviare,' I said.

'For one,' Cary said.

'What will you have? Smoked salmon?'

'You order yours,' Cary said.

I ordered '*bresse à l'estragon à la broche*', a little Roquefort, and some wild strawberries. This, I thought, was a moment too for the *Gruaud Larose* '34 (they would have learnt their lesson about the temperature). I leant back feeling pleased and contented: my dispute with the waiter was quite forgotten, and I knew that I had behaved politely and with moderation when I found that our table was occupied.

'And Madame?' the waiter asked.

'A roll and butter and a cup of coffee,' Cary said.

'But Madame perhaps would like . . .' She gave him her sweetest smile as though to show me what I had missed. She said, 'Just a roll and butter please. I'm not hungry. To keep Monsieur company.'

I said angrily, 'In *that* case I'll cancel . . .' but the waiter had already gone. I said, 'How dare you?'

'What's the matter, darling?'

'You know very well what's the matter. You let me order . . .'

'But truly I'm not hungry, darling. I just wanted to be sentimental, that's all. A roll and butter reminds me of the days when we weren't rich. Don't you remember that little café at the foot of the steps?'

'You are laughing at me.'

'But *no*, darling. Don't you like thinking of those days at all?'

'Those days, those days – why don't you talk about last week and how you were afraid to send anything to the laundry and we couldn't afford the English papers

172

and you couldn't read the French ones and . . .'

'Don't you remember how reckless you were when you gave five francs to a beggar? Oh, that reminds me . . .'

'What of?'

'I never meet the hungry young man now.'

'I don't suppose he goes sunbathing.'

My caviare came and my vodka. The waiter said, 'Would Madame like her coffee now?'

'No. No, I think I'll toy with it while Monsieur has his – his . . .'

'*Bresse à l'estragon*, Madame.'

I've never enjoyed caviare less. She watched every helping I took, her chin in her hand, leaning forward in what I suppose she meant to be a devoted and wifely way. The toast crackled in the silence, but I was determined not to be beaten. I ate the next course grimly to an end and pretended not to notice how she spaced out her roll – she couldn't have been enjoying her meal much either. She said to the waiter, 'I'll have another cup of coffee to keep my husband company with his strawberries. Wouldn't you like a half bottle of champagne, darling?'

'No. If I drink any more I might lose my self-control . . .'

'Darling, what have I said? Don't you like me to remember the days when we were poor and happy? After all, if I had married you now it might have been for your money. You know you were terribly nice when you gave me five hundred francs to gamble with. You watched the wheel so seriously.'

'Aren't I serious now?'

'You don't watch the wheel any longer. You watch

173

your paper and your figures. Darling, we are on *holiday*.'

'We would have been if Dreuther had come.'

'We can afford to go by ourselves now. Let's take a plane tomorrow – anywhere.'

'Not tomorrow. You see, according to my calculations the cycle of loss comes up tomorrow. Of course I'll only use 1,000-franc tokens, so as to reduce the incident.'

'Then the day after . . .'

'That's when I have to win back on double stakes. If you've finished your coffee it's time for the ballet.'

'I've got a headache. I don't want to go.'

'Of course you've got a headache eating nothing but rolls.'

'I ate nothing but rolls for three days and I never had a headache.' She got up from the table and said slowly, 'But in those days I was in love.' I refused to quarrel and I went to the ballet alone.

I can't remember which ballet it was – I don't know that I could have remembered even the same night. My mind was occupied. I had to lose next day if I were to win the day after, otherwise my system was at fault. My whole stupendous run would prove to have been luck only – the kind of luck that presumably by the laws of chance turns up in so many centuries, just as those long-lived laborious monkeys who are set at typewriters eventually in the course of centuries produce the works of Shakespeare. The ballerina to me was hardly a woman so much as a ball spinning on the wheel: when she finished her final movement and came before the curtain alone it was as though she had come to rest triumphantly at zero and all the counters around her were shovelled away into the back – the two thousand francs from the cheap seats with the square tokens from the stalls, all

174

jumbled together. I took a turn on the terrace to clear my head: this was where we had stood the first night watching together for the *Seagull*. I wished Cary had been with me and I nearly returned straight away to the hotel to give her all she asked. She was right: system or chance, who cared? We could catch a plane, extend our holiday: I had enough now to buy a partnership in some safe modest business without walls of glass and modern sculpture and a Gom on the eighth floor, and yet – it was like leaving a woman one loved untouched, untasted, to go away and never know the truth of how the ball had come to rest in that particular order – the poetry of absolute chance or the determination of a closed system? I would be grateful for the poetry, but what pride I should feel if I proved the determinism.

The regiment was all assembled: strolling by the tables I felt like a commanding officer inspecting his unit. I would have liked to reprove the old lady for wearing the artificial daisies askew on her hat and to speak sharply to Mr Bowles for a lack of polish on his ear-appliance. A touch on my elbow and I handed out my 200 token to the lady who cadged. 'Move more smartly to it,' I wanted to say to her, 'the arm should be extended at full length and not bent at the elbow, and it's time you did something about your hair.' They watched me pass with expressions of nervous regret, waiting for me to choose my table, and when I halted somebody rose and offered me a seat. But I had not come to win – I had come symbolically to make my first loss and go. So courteously I declined the seat, laid out a pattern of tokens and with a sense of triumph saw them shovelled away. Then I went back to the hotel.

Cary wasn't there, and I was disappointed. I wanted

to explain to her the importance of that symbolic loss, and instead I could only undress and climb between the humdrum sheets. I slept fitfully. I had grown used to Cary's company, and I put on the light at one to see the time, and I was still alone. At half past two Cary woke me as she felt her way to bed in the dark.

'Where've you been?' I asked.

'Walking,' she said.

'All by yourself?'

'No.' The space between the beds filled with her hostility, but I knew better than to strike the first blow – she was waiting for that advantage. I pretended to roll over and settle for sleep. After a long time she said, 'We walked down to the Sea Club.'

'It's closed.'

'We found a way in – it was very big and eerie in the dark with all the chairs stacked.'

'Quite an adventure. What did you do for light?'

'Oh, there was bright moonlight. Philippe told me all about his life.'

'I hope you unstacked a chair.'

'We sat on the floor.'

'If it was a madly interesting life tell it me. Otherwise it's late and I have to be . . .'

'"Up early for the Casino." I don't suppose you'd find it an interesting life. It was so simple, idyllic. And he told it with such intensity. He went to school at a *lycée*.'

'Most people do in France.'

'His parents died and he lived with his grandmother.'

'What about his grandfather?'

'He was dead too.'

'Senile mortality is very high in France.'

'He did military service for two years.'

I said, 'It certainly seems a life of striking originality.'

'You can sneer and sneer,' she said.

'But, dear, I've said nothing.'

'Of course you wouldn't be interested. You are never interested in anybody different from yourself, and he's young and very poor. He feeds on coffee and rolls.'

'Poor fellow,' I said with genuine sympathy.

'You are so uninterested you don't even ask his name.'

'You said it was Philippe.'

'Philippe who?' she asked triumphantly.

'Dupont,' I said.

'It isn't. It's Chantier.'

'Ah well, I mixed him up with Dupont.'

'Who's Dupont?'

'Perhaps they look alike.'

'I said who's Dupont.'

'I've no idea,' I said. 'But it's awfully late.'

'You're unbearable.' She slapped her pillow as though it were my face. There was a pause of several minutes and then she said bitterly, 'You haven't even asked whether I slept with him.'

'I'm sorry. Did you?'

'No. But he asked me to spend the night with him.'

'On the stacked chairs?'

'I'm having dinner with him tomorrow night.'

She was beginning to get me in the mood she wanted. I could stop myself no longer. I said, 'Who the hell is this Philippe Chantier?'

'The hungry young man, of course.'

'Are you going to dine on coffee and rolls?'

'I'm paying for the dinner. He's very proud, but I insisted. He's taking me somewhere very cheap and quiet and simple – a sort of students' place.'

'That's lucky,' I said, 'because I'm dining out too. Someone I met tonight at the Casino.'

'Who?'

'A Madame Dupont.'

'There's no such name.'

'I couldn't tell you the right one. I'm careful of a woman's honour.'

'Who is she?'

'She was winning a lot tonight at baccarat and we got into conversation. Her husband died recently, she was very fond of him, and she's sort of drowning her sorrows. I expect she'll soon find comfort, because she's young and beautiful and intelligent and rich.'

'Where are you having dinner?'

'Well, I don't want to bring her here – there might be talk. And she's too well known at the *Salle Privée*. She suggested driving to Cannes where nobody would know us.'

'Well, don't bother to come back early. I shall be late.'

'Exactly what I was going to say to you, dear.'

It was that sort of night. As I lay awake – and was aware of her wakefulness a few feet away – I thought it's the Gom's doing, he's even ruining our marriage now. I said, 'Dear, if you'll give up your dinner, I'll give up mine.'

She said, 'I don't even believe in yours. You invented it.'

'I swear to you – word of honour – that I'm giving a woman dinner tomorrow night.'

She said, 'I can't let Philippe down.' I thought gloomily: now I've got to do it, and where the hell can I find a woman?

[2]

We were very polite to each other at breakfast and at lunch. Cary even came into the Casino with me in the early evening, but I think her sole motive was to spot my woman. As it happened a young woman of great beauty was sitting at one of the tables, and Cary obviously drew the incorrect conclusion. She tried to see whether we exchanged glances and at last she could restrain her curiosity no longer. She said to me, 'Aren't you going to speak to her?'

'Who?'

'That girl.'

'I don't know what you mean,' I said, and tried to convey in my tone of voice that I was still guarding the honour of another. Cary said furiously, 'I must be off. I can't keep Philippe waiting. He's so sensitive.'

My system was working: I was losing exactly what I had anticipated losing, but all the exhilaration had gone out of my calculations. I thought: suppose this isn't what they call a lovers' quarrel; suppose she's really interested in this man; suppose this is the end. What do I do? What's left for me? Fifteen thousand pounds was an inadequate answer.

I was not the only one who was losing regularly. Mr Bowles sat in his wheeled chair, directing his nurse who put the tokens on the cloth for him, leaning over his shoulder, pushing with her private rake. He too had a system, but I suspected that his system was not working out. He sent her back twice to the desk for more money, and the second time I saw that his pocket-book was empty except for a few thousand-franc notes. He rapped out his directions and she laid out his remaining tokens –

a hundred and fifty thousand francs' worth of them – the ball rolled and he lost the lot. Wheeling from the table he caught sight of me. 'You,' he said, 'what's your name?'

'Bertram.'

'I've cashed too little. Don't want to go back to the hotel. Lend me five million.'

'I'm sorry,' I said.

'You know who I am. You know what I'm worth.'

'The hotel . . .' I began.

'They can't let me have that amount till the banks open. I want it tonight. You've been winning plenty. I've watched you. I'll pay you back before the evening's out.'

'People have been known to lose.'

'I can't hear what you say,' he said shifting his ear-piece.

'I'm sorry, Mr Other,' I said.

'My name's not Other. You know me. I'm A.N. Bowles.'

'We call you A.N.Other in the office. Why don't you go to the bank here and cash a cheque? There's someone always on duty.'

'I haven't got a French account, young man. Haven't you heard of currency regulations?'

'They don't seem to be troubling either of us much,' I said.

'You'd better come and have a cup of coffee and discuss the matter.'

'I'm busy just now.'

'Young man,' the Other said, 'I'm your employer.'

'I don't recognize anybody but the Gom.'

'Who on earth is the Gom?'

'Mr Dreuther.'

'The Gom. A.N.Other. There seems to be a curious lack of respect for the heads of your firm. Sir Walter Blixon – has he a name?'

'I believe the junior staff know him as the Blister.'

A thin smile momentarily touched the grey powdery features. 'At least that name is expressive,' A.N.Other remarked. 'Nurse, you can take a walk for half an hour. You can go as far as the harbour and back. You've always told me you like boats.'

When I turned the chair and began to push Bowles into the bar, a slight sweat had formed on my forehead and hands. An idea had come to me so fantastic that it drove away the thought of Cary and her hungry squire. I couldn't even wait till I got to the bar. I said, 'I've got fifteen million francs in my safe deposit box at the hotel. You can have them tonight in return for your shares.'

'Don't be a fool. They are worth twenty million at par, and Dreuther or Blixon would give me fifty million for them. A glass of Perrier water, please.'

I got him his water. He said, 'Now fetch me that five million.'

'No.'

'Young man,' he said, 'I have an infallible system. I have promised myself for twenty years to break the bank. I will not be foiled by a mere five million. Go and fetch them. Unless you do I shall order your dismissal.'

'Do you think that threat means anything to a man with fifteen million in the safe? And tomorrow I shall have twenty million.'

'You've been losing all tonight. I've watched you.'

'I had expected to lose. It proves my system's right.'

'There can't be two infallible systems.'

'Yours, I'm afraid, will prove only too fallible.'

'Tell me how yours works.'

'No. But I'll advise you on what is wrong with yours.'

'My system is my own.'

'How much have you won by it?'

'I have not yet begun to win. I am only at the first stage. Tonight I begin to win. Damn you, young man, fetch me that five million.'

'My system has won over fifteen million.'

I had got a false impression that the Other was a calm man. It is easy to appear calm when your movements are so confined. But when his fingers moved an inch on his knee he was exhibiting an uncontrollable emotion: his head swayed a minute degree and set the cord of his ear-appliance flapping. It was like the tiny stir of air clinking a shutter that is yet the sign of a tornado's approach.

He said, 'Suppose we have hit on the same system.'

'We haven't. I've been watching yours. I know it well. You can buy it in a paper packet at the stationer's for a thousand francs.'

'That's false. I thought it out myself, over the years, young man, in this chair. Twenty years of years.'

'It's not only *great* minds that think alike. But the bank will never be broken by a thousand-franc system marked on the envelope Infallible.'

'I'll prove you wrong. I'll make you eat that packet. Fetch me the five million.'

'I've told you my terms.'

Backward and forward and sideways moved the hands in that space to which illness confined him. They ran like mice in a cage – I could imagine them nibbling at the intolerable bars. 'You don't know what you are asking. Don't you realize you'd control the company if you chose to side with Blixon?'

'At least I would know something about the company controlled.'

'Listen. If you let me have the five million tonight, I will repay it in the morning and give you half my winnings.'

'There won't be any winnings with your system.'

'You seem very sure of yours.'

'Yes.'

'I might consider selling the shares for twenty million plus your system.'

'I haven't got twenty million.'

'Listen, if you are so sure of yourself you can take an option on the shares for fifteen million now. You pay the balance in twenty-four hours – 9 p.m. tomorrow – or you forfeit your fifteen million. In addition you give me your system.'

'It's a crazy proposal.'

'This is a crazy place.'

'If I don't win five million tomorrow, I don't have a single share?'

'Not a single share.' The fingers had stopped moving.

I laughed. 'Doesn't it occur to you that I've only got to phone the office tomorrow, and Blixon would advance me the money on the option? He wants the shares.'

'Tomorrow is Sunday and the agreement is for cash.'

'I don't give you the system till the final payment,' I said.

'I shan't want it if you've lost.'

'But I need money to play with.'

He took that carefully in. I said, 'You can't run a system on a few thousand francs.'

'You can pay ten million now,' he said, 'on account of fifteen. If you lose, you'll owe me five million.'

'How would you get it?'

He gave me a malign grin. 'I'll have your wages docked five hundred a year for ten years.'

I believe he meant it. In the world of Dreuther and Blixon he and his small packet of shares had survived only by the hardness, the meanness and the implacability of his character.

'I shall have to win ten million with five million.'

'You said you had the perfect system.'

'I thought I had.'

The old man was bitten by his own gamble: he jeered at me. 'Better just lend me the five million and forget the option.'

I thought of the Gom at sea in his yacht with his headline guests and the two of us forgotten – what did he care about his assistant accountant? I remembered the way he had turned to Miss Bullen and said, 'Arrange for Mr Bertrand (he couldn't bother to get my name right) to be married.' Would he arrange through Miss Bullen for our children to be born and our parents to be buried? I thought, with these shares at Blixon's call I shall have him fixed – he'll be powerless, I'll be employing him for just as long as I want him to feel the sting: then no more room on the eighth floor, no more yacht, no more of his '*luxe, calme et volupté*'. He had taken me in with his culture and his courtesy and his phoney kindness until I had nearly accepted him for the great man he believed himself to be. Now, I thought with a sadness for which I couldn't account, he will be small enough to be in my hands, and I looked at my ink-stained fingers with disrelish.

'You see,' the Other said, 'you don't believe any longer.'

'Oh, yes, I do,' I said, 'I'll take your bet. I was just thinking of something else – that's all.'

[3]

I went and fetched the money and we drew up the option right away on a sheet of notepaper and the nurse – who had returned by then – and the barman witnessed it. The option was to be taken up at 9 p.m. prompt in the same spot next day: the Other didn't want his gambling to be interrupted before his dinner-hour whether by good or bad news. Then I made him buy me a glass of whisky, though Moses had less trouble in extracting his drink from a rock in Sinai, and I watched him being pushed back to the *Salle Privée*. To all intents and purposes, for the next twenty-four hours, I was the owner of Sitra. Neither Dreuther nor Blixon in their endless war could make a move without the consent of their assistant accountant. It was strange to think that neither was aware of how the control of the business had changed – from a friend of Dreuther to an enemy of Dreuther. Blixon would be down in Hampshire reading up tomorrow's lessons, polishing up his pronunciation of the names in Judges – he would feel no exhilaration. And Dreuther – Dreuther was at sea, out of reach, playing bridge probably with his social lions – he would not be touched by the sense of insecurity. I ordered another whisky: I no longer doubted my system and I had no sense of regret. Blixon would be the first to hear: I would telephone to the office on Monday morning. It would be tactful to inform him of the new position through my chief, Arnold. There must be no temporary *rapprochement* between Dreuther and Blixon against the intruder: I would have Arnold explain to Blixon that for the time being he could count on me. Dreuther would not even hear of the matter unless he rang up his office from some port of call. Even that I could prevent: I could tell Arnold that the secret must be kept till Dreuther's return, for then I would have the pleasure of giving him the information in person.

I went out to tell Cary the news, forgetting about our engagements: I wanted to see her face when I told her she was the wife of the man who controlled the company. You've hated my system, I wanted to say to her, and the hours I have spent at the Casino, but there was no vulgar cause – it wasn't money I was after, and I quite forgot that until that evening I had no other motive than money. I began to believe that I had planned this from the first two-hundred-franc bet in the *cuisine*.

But of course there was no Cary to be found – 'Madame went out with a gentleman,' the porter needlessly told me, and I remembered the date at the simple students' café. Well, there had been a time in my life when I had found little difficulty in picking up a woman and I went back to the Casino to fulfil my word. But the beautiful woman had got a man with her now: their fingers nuzzled over their communal tokens, and I soon realized that single women who came to the Casino to gamble were seldom either beautiful or interested in men. The ball and not the bed was the focal point. I thought of Cary's questions and my own lies – and there wasn't a lie she wouldn't see through.

I watched Bird's Nest circling among the tables, making a quick pounce here and there, out of the croupier's eye. She had a masterly technique: when a pile was large enough she would lay her fingers on a single piece and give a tender ogle at the owner as much as to say, 'You are so generous and I am all yours for the taking.' She was so certain of her own appeal that no one had the heart to expose her error. Tonight she was wearing long amber ear-rings and a purple evening dress that exposed her best feature – her shoulders. Her shoulders were magnificent, wide and animal, but then, like a revolving light, her face inevitably came round, the untidy false blonde hair tangled up with the ear-rings (I am sure she thought of her wisps and strands as 'wanton locks'), and that smile fixed like a fossil. Watching her revolve I began to revolve too: I was caught into her orbit, and I became aware that here alone was the answer. I had to dine with a woman and in the whole Casino this was the only woman who would dine with me. As she swerved away from an attendant with a sweep of drapery and a slight clank, clank from her evening bag where I supposed she had stowed her hundred-franc tokens, I touched her hand. 'Dear lady,' I said – the phrase astonished me: it was as though it had been placed on my tongue, and certainly it seemed to belong to the same period as the mauve evening dress, the magnificent shoulders. 'Dear lady,' I repeated with increasing astonishment (I almost expected a small white moustache to burgeon on my upper lip), 'you will I trust excuse a stranger . . .'

I think she must have gone in constant fear of the attendants because her instinctive ogle expanded with her relief at seeing me into a positive blaze of light: it flapped across the waste of her face like sheet lightning. 'Oh, not a stranger,' she said, and I was relieved to find that she was English and that at least I would not have to talk bad French throughout the evening. 'I have been watching with such admiration your great good fortune.' (She had indeed profited from it on several occasions.)

'I was wondering, dear lady,'(the extraordinary phrase slipped out again) 'if you would do me the honour of dining. I have no one with whom to celebrate my luck.'

'But, of course, colonel, it would be a great pleasure.' At that I really put my hand up to my mouth to see if the moustache were there. We both seemed to have learnt parts in a play – I began to fear what the third act might hold. I noticed she was edging towards the restaurant of the *Salle Privée*, but all my snobbery revolted at dining there with so notorious a figure of fun. I said, 'I thought perhaps – if we could take a little air – it's such a beautiful evening, the heat of these rooms, some small exclusive place . . .' I would have suggested a private room if I had not feared that my intentions might have been misunderstood and welcomed.

'Nothing would give me greater pleasure, colonel.'

We swept out (there was no other word for it) and I prayed that Cary and her young man were safely at dinner in their cheap café; it would have been intolerable if she had seen me at that moment. The woman imposed unreality. I was persuaded that to the white moustache had now been added a collapsible opera hat and a scarlet lined cloak.

I said, 'A horse-cab, don't you think, on a night so balmy . . .'

'Barmy, colonel?'

'Spelt with an L,' I explained, but I don't think she understood.

When we were seated in the cab I appealed for her help. 'I am really quite a stranger here. I have dined out so seldom. Where can we go that is quiet . . . and exclusive?' I was determined that the place should be exclusive: if it excluded all the world but the two of us, I would be the less embarrassed.

'There is a small new restaurant – a club really, very *comme il faut*. It is called *Orphée*. Rather expensive, I fear, colonel.'

'Expense is no object.' I gave the name to the driver and leant back. As she was sitting bolt upright I was able to shelter behind her bulk. I said, 'When were you last in Cheltenham . . . ?'

The devil was about us that night. Whatever I said had been written into my part. She replied promptly, 'Dear Cheltenham . . . how did you discover . . . ?'

'Well, you know, a handsome woman catches one's eye.'

'You live there too?'

'One of those little houses off Queen's Parade.'

'We must be near neighbours,' and to emphasize our nearness I could feel her massive flank move ever so slightly against me. I was glad that the cab drew up: we hadn't gone more than two hundred yards from the Casino.

'A bit highbrow, what?' I said, glaring up as I felt a colonel should do at the lit mask above the door made out of an enormous hollowed potato. We had to brush our way through shreds of cotton which were meant, I suppose, to represent cobwebs. The little room inside was hung with photographs of authors, actors and film stars, and we had to sign our name in a book, thus apparently becoming life members of the club. I wrote

Robert Devereux. I could feel her leaning against my shoulder, squinnying at the signature.

The restaurant was crowded and rather garishly lit by bare globes. There were a lot of mirrors that must have been bought at the sale of some old restaurant, for they advertised ancient specialities like 'Mutton Chopps'.

She said, 'Cocteau was at the opening.'

'Who's he?'

'Oh, colonel,' she said, 'you are laughing at me.'

I said, 'Oh well, you know, in my kind of life one hasn't much time for books,' and suddenly, just under the word Chopps, I saw Cary gazing back at me.

'How I envy a life of action,' my companion said, and laid down her bag – chinkingly – on the table. The whole bird's nest shook and the amber ear-rings swung as she turned to me and said confidingly, 'Tell me, colonel. I love – passionately – to hear men talk of their lives.' (Cary's eyes in the mirror became enormous: her mouth was a little open as though she had been caught in mid-sentence.)

I said, 'Oh well, there's not much to tell.'

'Men are so much more modest than women. If I had deeds of derring-do to my credit I would never tire of telling them. Cheltenham must seem very quiet to you.' I heard a spoon drop at a neighbouring table. I said weakly, 'Oh well, I don't mind quiet. What will you eat?'

'I have such a teeny-weeny appetite, colonel. A *langouste thermidor* . . .'

'And a bottle of the Widow?' I could have bitten my tongue – the hideous words were out before I could stop them. I wanted to turn to Cary and say, 'This isn't me. I didn't write this. It's my part. Blame the author.'

A voice I didn't know said, 'But I adore you. I adore everything you do, the way you talk, the way you are so silent. I wish I could speak English much much better so that I could tell you . . .' I turned slowly sideways and looked at Cary. I had never, since I kissed her first, seen so complete a blush. Bird's Nest said, 'So young and so romantic, aren't they? I always think the English are too reticent. That's what makes our encounter so strange. Half an hour ago we didn't even know each other, and now here we are with – what did you call it? – a bottle of the Widow. How I love these masculine phrases. Are you married, colonel?'

'Well, in a way . . .'

'How do you mean?'

'We're sort of separated.'

'How sad. I'm separated too – by death. Perhaps that's less sad.'

A voice I had begun to detest said, 'Your husband does not deserve you to be faithful. To leave you all night while he gambles . . .'

'He's not gambling tonight,' Cary said. She added in a strangled voice, 'He's in Cannes having dinner with a young, beautiful, intelligent widow.'

'Don't cry, *chérie*.'

'I'm not crying, Philippe. I'm, I'm, I'm laughing. If he could see me now . . .'

'He would be wild with jealousy, I hope. Are you jealous?'

'So touching,' Bird's Nest said. 'One can't help listening. One seems to glimpse an entire life . . .'

The whole affair seemed to me abominably one-sided. 'Women are so gullible,' I said, raising my voice a little. 'My wife started going around with a young man because he looked hungry. Perhaps he was hungry. He would take her to expensive restaurants like this and make her pay. Do you know what they charge for a *langouste thermidor* here? It's so expensive, they don't even put the price on the bill. A simple inexpensive café for students.'

'I don't understand, colonel. Has something upset you?'

'And the wine. Don't you think I had to draw the line at his drinking wine at my expense?'

'You must have been treated shamefully.'

Somebody put down a glass so hard that it broke. The detestable voice said, '*Chérie*, that is good fortune for us. Look – I put some wine behind your ears, on the top of your head . . . Do you think your husband will sleep with the beautiful lady in Cannes?'

'Sleep is about all he's capable of doing.'

I got to my feet and shouted at her – I could stand no more. 'How dare you say such things?'

'Philippe,' Cary said, 'let's go.' She put some notes on the table and led him out. He was too surprised to object.

Bird's Nest said, 'They were really going too far, weren't they? Talking like that in public. I love your old-fashioned chivalry, colonel. The young must learn.'

She took nearly an hour before she got through her *langouste thermidor* and her strawberry ice. She began to tell me the whole story of her life, beginning over the *langouste* with a childhood in an old rectory in Kent and ending over the ice-cream with her small widow's portion at Cheltenham. She was staying in a little *pension* in Monte Carlo because it was 'select', and I suppose her methods at the Casino very nearly paid for her keep.

I got rid of her at last and went home. I was afraid that

Cary wouldn't be there, but she was sitting up in bed reading one of those smart phrase books that are got up like a novel and are terribly bright and gay. When I opened the door she looked up over the book and said, '*Entrez, mon colonel.*'

'What are you reading that for?' I said.

'*J'essaye de faire mon français un peu meilleur.*'

'Why?'

'I might live in France one day.'

'Oh? Who with? The hungry student?'

'Philippe has asked me to marry him.'

'After what his dinner must have cost you tonight, I suppose he had to take an honourable line.'

'I told him there was a temporary impediment.'

'You mean your bad French?'

'I meant you, of course.'

Suddenly she began to cry, burying her head under the phrase book so that I shouldn't see. I sat down on the bed and put my hand on her side: I felt tired: I felt we were very far from the public house at the corner: I felt we had been married a long time and it hadn't worked. I had no idea how to pick up the pieces – I have never been good with my hands.

I said, 'Let's go home.'

'Not wait any more for Mr Dreuther?'

'Why should we? I practically own Mr Dreuther now.'

I hadn't meant to tell her, but out it came, all of it. She emerged from under the phrase book and she stopped crying. I told her that when I had extracted the last fun out of being Dreuther's boss, I would sell my shares at a good profit to Blixon – and that would be the final end of Dreuther. 'We'll be comfortably off,' I said.

'*We* won't.'

'What do you mean?'

'Darling, I'm not hysterical now and I'm not angry. I'm talking really seriously. I didn't marry a well-off man. I married a man I met in the bar of the Volunteer – someone who liked cold sausages and travelled by bus because taxis were too expensive. He hadn't had a very good life. He married a bitch who ran away from him. I wanted – oh, enormously – to give him fun. Now suddenly I've woken up in bed with a man who can buy all the fun he wants and his idea of fun is to ruin an old man who was kind to him. What if Dreuther did forget he'd invited you? He meant it at the time. He looked at you and you seemed tired and he liked you – just like that, for no reason, just as I liked you the first time in the Volunteer. That's how human beings work. They don't work on a damned system like your roulette.'

'The system hasn't done so badly for you.'

'Oh yes, it has. It's destroyed me. I've lived for you and now I've lost you.'

'You haven't. I'm here.'

'When I return home and go into the bar of the Volunteer, you won't be there. When I'm waiting at the 19 bus stop you won't be there either. You won't be anywhere where *I* can find you. You'll be driving down to your place in Hampshire like Sir Walter Blixon. Darling, you've been very lucky and you've won a lot of money, but I don't like you any more.'

I sneered back at her, but there wasn't any heart in my sneer. 'You only love the poor, I suppose?'

'Isn't that better than only loving the rich? Darling, I'm going to sleep on the sofa in the sitting-room.' We had a sitting-room again now, and a dressing-room for

194

me, just as at the beginning. I said, 'Don't bother. I've got my own bed.'

I went out on to the balcony. It was like the first night when we had quarrelled, but this time she didn't come out on to her balcony, and we hadn't quarrelled. I wanted to knock on her door and say something, but I didn't know what words to use. All my words seemed to chink like the tokens in Bird's Nest's bag.

[4]

I didn't see her for breakfast, nor for lunch. I went into the Casino after lunch and for the first time I didn't want to win. But the devil was certainly in my system and win I did. I had the money to pay Bowles, I owned the shares, and I wished I had lost my last two hundred francs in the kitchen. After that I walked along the terrace – sometimes one gets ideas walking, but I didn't. And then looking down into the harbour I saw a white boat which hadn't been there before. She was flying the British flag and I recognized her from newspaper photographs. She was the *Seagull*. The Gom had come after all – he wasn't much more than a week late. I thought, you bastard, if only you'd troubled to keep your promise, I wouldn't have lost Cary. I wasn't important enough for you to remember and now I'm too important for her to love. Well, if I've lost her, you are going to lose everything too – Blixon will probably buy your boat.

I walked into the bar and the Gom was there. He had just ordered himself a Pernod and he was talking with easy familiarity to the barman, speaking perfect French. Whatever the man's language he would have spoken it perfectly – he was of the Pentecostal type. Yet he wasn't the Dreuther of the eighth floor now – he had put an old yachting cap on the bar, he had several days' growth of white beard and he wore an old and baggy pair of blue trousers and a sweat shirt. When I came in he didn't stop talking, but I could see him examining me in the mirror behind the bar. He kept on glancing at me as though I pricked a memory. I realized that he had not only forgotten his invitation, he had even forgotten me.

'Mr Dreuther,' I said.

He turned as slowly as he could; he was obviously trying to remember.

'You don't remember me,' I said.

'Oh, my dear chap, I remember you perfectly. Let me see, the last time we met . . .'

'My name's Bertram.' I could see it didn't mean a thing to him. He said, 'Of course. Of course. Been here long?'

'We arrived about nine days ago. We hoped you'd be in time for our wedding.'

'Wedding?' I could see it all coming back to him and for a moment he was foxed for an explanation.

'My dear chap, I hope everything was all right. We were caught with engine trouble. Out of touch. You know how it can be at sea. Now you are coming on board tonight, I hope. Get your bags packed. I want to sail at midnight. Monte Carlo is too much of a temptation for me. How about you? Been losing money?' He was sweeping his mistake into limbo on a tide of words.

'No, I've gained a little.'

'Hang on to it. It's the only way.' He was rapidly paying for his Pernod – he wanted to get away from his mistake as quickly as possible. 'Follow me down. We'll eat on board tonight. The three of us. No one else joins the boat until Portofino. Tell them I'll settle the bill.'

'It's not necessary. I can manage.'

'I can't have you out of pocket because I'm late.' He snatched his yachting cap and was gone. I could almost imagine he had a seaman's lurch. He had given me no time to develop my hatred or even to tell him that I didn't know where my wife was. I put the money for Bowles in an envelope and asked the porter to have it waiting for him in the bar of the Casino at nine. Then I went upstairs and began to pack my bags. I had a wild hope that if I could get Cary to sea our whole trouble might be left on shore in the luxury hotel, in the great ornate *Salle Privée*. I would have liked to stake all our troubles *en plein* and to lose them. It was only when I had finished my packing and went into her room that I knew I hadn't a hope. The room was more than empty – it was vacant. It was where somebody had been and wouldn't be again. The dressing-table was waiting for another user – the only thing left was the conventional letter. Women read so many magazines – they know the formula for parting. I think they have even learned the words by heart from the glossy pages – they are impersonal. 'Darling, I'm off. I couldn't bear to tell you that and what's the use ? We don't fit any more.' I thought of nine days ago and how we'd urged the old horse-cab on. Yes, they said at the desk, Madame had checked out an hour ago.

I told them to keep my bags. Dreuther wouldn't want me to stay on board after what I was going to tell him.

[5]

Dreuther had shaved and changed his shirt and was reading a book in his little lounge. He again had the grand air of the eighth floor. The bar stood hospitably open and the flowers looked as though they had been newly arranged. I wasn't impressed. I knew about his kindness, but kindness at the skin-deep level can ruin people. Kindness has got to care. I carried a knife in my mind and waited to use it.

'But your wife has not come with you?'

'She'll be following,' I said.

'And your bags?'

'The bags too. Could I have a drink?'

I had no compunction in gaining the Dutch courage for assassination at his own expense. I had two whiskies very quickly. He poured them out himself, got the ice, served me like an equal. And he had no idea that in fact I was his superior.

'You look tired,' he said. 'The holiday has not done you good.'

'I have worries.'

'Did you remember to bring the Racine?'

'Yes.' I was momentarily touched that he had remembered that detail.

'Perhaps after dinner you would read a little. I was once fond of him like you. There is so much that I have forgotten. Age is a great period of forgetting.' I remembered what Cary had said – after all, at his age, hadn't he a right to forget? But when I thought of Cary I could have cried into my glass.

'We forget a lot of things near at hand, but we remember the past. I am often troubled by the past. Unnecessary misunderstanding. Unnecessary pain.'

'Could I have another whisky?'

'Of course.' He got up promptly to serve me. Leaning over his little bar, with his wide patriarchal back turned to me, he said, 'Do not mind talking. We are not on the eighth floor now. Two men on holiday. Friends I hope. Drink. There is no harm, if one is unhappy, in being a little drunk.'

I was a little drunk – more than a little. I couldn't keep my voice steady when I said, 'My wife isn't coming. She's left me.'

'A quarrel?'

'Not a real quarrel. Not words you can deny or forget.'

'Is she in love with someone else?'

'I don't know. Perhaps.'

'Tell me. I can't help. But one needs a listener.' Using the pronoun 'one' he made mine a general condition from which all men were destined to suffer. 'One' is born, 'one' dies, 'one' loses love. I told him everything – except what I had come to the boat to tell him. I told him of our coffee-and-roll lunches, of my winnings, of the hungry student and the Bird's Nest. I told him of our words over the waiter, I told him of her simple statement, 'I don't like you any more.' I even (it seems incredible to me now) showed him her letter.

He said, 'I am very sorry. If I had not been – delayed, this would not have happened. On the other hand you would not have won all this money.'

I said, 'Damn the money.'

'That is very easy to say. I have said it so often myself. But here I am –' he waved his hand round the little modest saloon that it took a very rich man to afford. 'If I had meant what I said, I wouldn't be here.'

'I do mean it.'

'Then you have hope.'

'She may be sleeping with him at this moment.'

'That does not destroy hope. So often one has

discovered how much one loves by sleeping with another.'

'What shall I do?'

'Have a cigar.'

'I don't like them.'

'You will not mind –' He lit one himself. 'These too cost money. Certainly I do not like money – who could? The coins are badly designed and the paper is unclean. Like newspapers picked up in a public park, but I like cigars, this yacht, hospitality, and I suppose, I am afraid, yes,' he added lowering his cigar-point like a flag, 'power.' I had even forgotten that he no longer had it. 'One has to put up with this money.'

'Do you know where they will be?' he asked me.

'Celebrating, I imagine – on coffee and rolls.'

'I have had four wives. Are you sure you want her back?'

'Yes.'

'It can be very peaceful without them.'

'I'm not looking for peace – yet.'

'My second wife – I was still young then – she left me, and I made the mistake of winning her back. It took me years to lose her again after that. She was a good woman. It is not easy to lose a good woman. If one must marry it is better to marry a bad woman.'

'I did the first time and it wasn't much fun.'

'How interesting.' He took a long pull and watched the smoke drift and dissolve. 'Still, it didn't last. A good woman lasts. Blixon is married to a good woman. She sits next to him in the pew on Sundays, thinking about the menu for dinner. She is an excellent housekeeper and has great taste in interior decoration. Her hands are plump – she says proudly that they are good pastry hands – but that is not what a woman's hands should be

200

for. She is a moral woman and when he leaves her during the week, he feels quite secure. But he has to go back, that is the terrible thing, he has to go back.'

'Cary isn't that good.' I looked at the last of my whisky. 'I wish to hell you could tell me what to do.'

'I am too old and the young would call me cynical. People don't like reality. They don't like common sense. Until age forces it on them. I would say – bring your bags, forget the whole matter – my whisky supply is large, for a few days anaesthetize yourself. I have some most agreeable guests coming on board tomorrow at Portofino – you will like Celia Charteris very much. At Naples there are several bordels if you find celibacy difficult. I will telephone to the office extending your leave. Be content with adventure. And don't try to domesticate adventure.'

I said, 'I want Cary. That's all. Not adventure.'

'My second wife left me because she said I was too ambitious. She didn't realize that it is only the dying who are free from ambition. And they probably have the ambition to live. Some men disguise their ambition – that's all. I was in a position to help this young man my wife loved. He soon showed his ambition then. There are different types of ambition – that is all, and my wife found she preferred mine. Because it was limitless. They do not feel the infinite as an unworthy rival, but for a man to prefer the desk of an assistant manager – that is an insult.' He looked mournfully at his long cigar-ash. 'All the same one should not meddle.'

'I would do anything . . .'

'Your wife is romantic. This young man's poverty appeals to her. I think I see a plan. Help yourself to another drink while I tell it to you . . .'

PART THREE

[1]

I went down the gang-plank, swaying slightly from the effect of the whisky, and walked up the hill from the port. It was a quarter past eight, and the sight of a clock reminded me for the first time of what I had not told Dreuther. Dreuther had said, 'Don't use money. Money is so obviously sordid. But those little round scarlet disks . . . You will see, no gambler can resist them.' I went to the Casino and looked for the pair: they were not there. Then I changed all the spare money I had, and when I came out my pocket clinked like Bird's Nest's bag.

It took me only a quarter of an hour to find them: they were in the café where we used to go for our meals. I watched them for a little, unseen from the door. Cary didn't look happy. She had gone there, she told me later, to prove to herself that she no longer loved me, that no sentiment attached to the places where we had been together, and she found that the proof didn't work out. She was miserable to see a stranger sitting in my chair, and the stranger had a habit she detested – he stuffed the roll into his mouth and bit off the buttered end. When he had finished he counted his resources and then asked her if she would mind not talking for a minute while he checked his system. 'We can go up to five hundred francs tonight in the kitchen,' he said, 'that is five one-hundred-franc stakes.' He was sitting there with a pencil and paper when I arrived.

I said 'Hullo,' from the doorway and Cary turned. She nearly smiled at me from habit – I could see the smile sailing up in her eyes and then she plucked it down like a boy might pluck his kite back to earth, out of the wind.

'What are you doing here?' she said.

'I wanted to make sure you were all right.'

'I am all right.'

'Sometimes one does something and wishes one hadn't.'

'Not me.'

'I wish you'd be quiet,' the young man said. 'What I am working out is very complicated.'

'Philippe, it's – my husband.'

He looked up, 'Oh, good evening,' and began to tap nervously on the table with the end of his pencil.

'I hope you are looking after my wife properly.'

'That's nothing to do with you,' he said.

'There are certain things you ought to know in order to make her happy. She hates skin on hot milk. Look, her saucer's full of scraps. You should attend to that before you pour out. She hates small sharp noises – for instance, the crackle of toast – or that roll you are eating. You must never chew nuts either. I hope you are listening. That noise with the pencil will not please her.'

'I wish you would go away,' the young man said.

'I would rather like to talk to my wife alone.'

'I don't want to be alone with you,' Cary said.

'You heard her. Please go.' It was strange how cleverly Dreuther had forecast our dialogue. I began to have hope.

'I'm sorry. I must insist.'

'You've no right . . .'

Cary said, 'Unless you leave us, we'll both walk out of here. Philippe, pay the bill.'

'*Chérie*, I do want to get my system straight.'

'I tell you what I'll do,' I said. 'I'm a much older man than you are, but I'll offer to fight you. If I win, I talk to Cary alone. If you win, I go away and never trouble you again.'

'I won't have you fighting,' Cary said.

'You heard her.'

'Alternatively, I'll pay for half an hour with her.'

'How dare you?' Cary said.

I put my hand in my pocket and pulled out fistfuls of yellow and red tokens – five-hundred-franc tokens, thousand-franc tokens, shooting them out on to the table between the coffee cups. He couldn't keep his eyes off them. They covered his system. I said, 'I'd rather fight. This is all the money I've got left.'

He stared at them. He said, 'I don't want to brawl.'

Cary said, 'Philippe, you wouldn't . . .'

I said, 'It's the only way you can get out of here without fighting.'

'*Chérie*, he only wants half an hour. After all, it's his right. There are things for you to settle together, and with this money I can really prove my system.'

She said to him in a voice to which in the past week I had become accustomed, 'All right. Take his money. Get along into that damned Casino. You've been thinking of nothing else all the evening.'

He had just enough grace to hesitate. 'I'll see you in half an hour, *chérie*.'

I said, 'I promise I'll bring her to the Casino myself. I have something to do there.' Then I called him back from the door, 'You've dropped a piece,' and he came back and felt for it under the table. Watching Cary's face I almost wished I hadn't won.

She was trying hard not to cry. She said, 'I suppose you think you've been very clever.'

'No.'

'You exposed him all right. You've demonstrated your point. What do I do now?'

'Come on board for one night. You've got a separate cabin. We can put you off in Genoa tomorrow.'

'I suppose you hope I'll change my mind?'

'Yes. I hope. It's not a very big hope, but it's better than despair. You see, I love you.'

'Would you promise never to gamble again?'

'Yes.'

'Would you throw away that damned system?'

'Yes.'

There was a song when I was young – 'and then my heart stood still'. That was what I felt when she began to make conditions. 'Have you told him,' she asked, 'about the shares?'

'No.'

'I can't go on that boat with him not knowing. It would be too mean.'

'I promise I'll clear it up – before sleep.'

She had her head lowered, so that I couldn't see her face, and she sat very silent. I had used all my arguments: there was nothing more for me to say either. The night was full of nothing but clinking cups and running water. At last she said, 'What are we waiting for?'

We picked up all the bags and then we walked across to the Casino. She hadn't wanted to come, but I said, 'I promised to bring you.' I left her in the hall and went through to the kitchen – he wasn't there. Then I went to the bar, and then on to the *Salle Privée*. There he was, playing for the first time with a 500-franc minimum. A.N. Other was at the same table – the five-thousand squares littered the table around him. He sat in his chair with his fingers moving like mice. I leant over his shoulder and gave him *his* news, but he made no sign of interest, for the ball was bouncing now around the wheel. It came to rest in zero as I reached Philippe and the bank raked in their winnings.

I said to Philippe, 'Cary's here. I kept my promise.'

'Tell her not to come in. I am winning – except the last round. I do not want to be disturbed.'

'She won't disturb you ever again.'

'I have won 10,000.'

'But it's loser takes all,' I said. 'Lose these for me. It's all I've got left.'

I didn't wait for him to protest – and i don't think he would have protested.

[2]

The Gom that night was a perfect host. He showed himself so ignorant of our trouble that we began to forget it ourselves. There were cocktails before dinner and champagne at dinner and I could see that Cary was getting a little uncertain in her choice of words. She went to bed early because she wanted to leave me alone with the Gom. We both came out on to the deck to say good night to her. A small breeze went by, tasting of the sea, and the clouds hid moon and stars and made the riding lights on the yachts shine the brighter.

The Gom said, 'Tomorrow night you shall persuade me that Racine is the greatest poet, but tonight let me think of Baudelaire.' He leant on the rail and recited in a low voice, and I wondered to whom it was in the past that the old wise man with limitless ambitions was speaking.

> '*Vois sur ces canaux*
> *Dormir ces vaisseaux*
> *Dont l'humeur est vagabonde;*
> *C'est pour asssouvir*
> *Ton moindre désir*
> *Qu'ils viennent du bout du monde.*'

He turned and said, 'I am speaking that to you, my dear, from him,' and he put his arm around her shoulder, and then gave her a push towards the companion-way. She gave a sound like a small animal in pain and was gone.

'What was the matter?' the Gom asked.

'She was remembering something.' I knew what it was she was remembering, but I didn't tell him.

We went back into the saloon and the Gom poured out our drinks. He said, 'I'm glad the trick worked.'

'She may still decide to get off at Genoa.'

'She won't. In any case we'll leave out Genoa.' He added thoughtfully, 'It's not the first time I've kidnapped a woman.'

He gave me my glass. 'I shan't keep you up drinking tonight, but I wanted to tell you something. I'm getting a new assistant accountant.'

'You mean – you are giving me notice?'

'Yes.'

Unpredictable, the old bastard, I thought – to tell me this now, as his guest. Could it be that in my absence he had met and spoken with the Other? He said, 'You'll need a bigger income now you are married. I'm putting Arnold in charge of General Enterprises. You are to be chief accountant in his place. Drink your whisky and go to bed. They are getting up the anchor now.'

When I went down I wondered whether Cary's cabin would be locked, but it wasn't. She sat on one bunk with her knees drawn up to her chin staring through the porthole. The engines had started and we were moving out. The lights of the port wheeled around the wall. She said, 'Have you told him?'

'No.'

'You promised,' she said. 'I can't go sailing down Italy in this boat with him not knowing. He's been so terribly kind . . .'

'I owe him everything,' I said. 'It was he who told me how to act to get you back. The trick was his. I could think of nothing. I was in despair.'

'Then you must tell him. Now. At once.'

'There's nothing to tell. You don't think after he'd done that for me, I'd cheat him with Blixon?'

'But the shares?'

'When I went to find Philippe, I took back the money I'd left for the Other. The option's forfeited. The Other's fifteen million richer – and Philippe has our last five million if he hasn't lost it. We are back where we were.' The words were the wrong ones. I said, 'If only we could be.'

'We never can be.'

'Never?'

'I love you so much more. Because I've been terribly mean to you and nearly lost you.'

We said very little for a long time: there was no room for anything but our bodies in the cramped berth, but some time towards morning, when the circle of the port-hole was grey, I woke her and told her what the Gom had said to me. 'We shan't be rich,' I added quickly for fear of losing her again, 'but we can afford Bournemouth next year . . .'

'No,' she said sleepily. 'Let's go to Le Touquet. They have a Casino there. But don't let's have a system.'

There was a promise I'd forgotten. I got up and took the great system out of my jacket-pocket and tore it in little pieces and threw them through the porthole – the white scraps blew back in our wake.

The sleepy voice said, 'Darling, it's terribly cold. It's snowing.'

'I'll close the porthole.'

'No. Just come back.'